Who is Lila kidding?

"I love you soooooooo," Lila sang in front of the mirror. She held on to the last, long, liquid note of the song.

The voice that filled the room was high and clear. It sounded perfect, beautiful.

The only trouble was, it was Johanna's voice. On tape.

Lila was lip-syncing.

She went over to her tape player and flipped it off with a sigh. Then she sat down on her bed and groaned. "Who am I kidding?" she wailed out loud. "I'll never be able to sing this song."

She closed her eyes and shuddered, thinking of all the bragging she had done. If she backed out now, or made a fool of herself by trying to sing, she'd never live it down.

Bantam Skylark Books in the SWEET VALLEY TWINS AND FRIENDS series.
Ask your bookseller for the books you have missed.

SWEET VALLEY TWINS
AND FRIENDS

Lila's
Music Video

Written by
Jamie Suzanne

Created by
FRANCINE PASCAL

A BANTAM SKYLARK BOOK ®
NEW YORK·TORONTO·LONDON·SYDNEY·AUCKLAND

RL 4, 008-012

LILA'S MUSIC VIDEO

A Bantam Skylark Book / October 1993

*Sweet Valley High® and Sweet Valley Twins and Friends® are
registered trademarks of Francine Pascal*

Conceived by Francine Pascal

*Produced by Daniel Weiss Associates, Inc.
33 West 17th Street
New York, NY 10011*

Cover art by James Mathewuse

*Skylark Books is a registered trademark of Bantam Books, a division of
Bantam Doubleday Dell Publishing Group, Inc.
Registered in U.S. Patent and Trademark Office and elsewhere.*

ISBN: 0-553-48059-6

Published simultaneously in the United States and Canada

*Bantam Books are published by Bantam Books, a division of Bantam
Doubleday Dell Publishing Group, Inc. Its trademark, consisting of the
words "Bantam Books" and the portrayal of a rooster, is Registered in
U.S. Patent and Trademark Office and in other countries. Marca
Registrada. Bantam Books, 1540 Broadway, New York, New York 10036.*

PRINTED IN THE UNITED STATES OF AMERICA

OPM   0 9 8 7 6 5 4 3 2 1

Lila's
Music Video

One

"I *love* RockTV," Tamara Chase said on Sunday afternoon, reaching for the bowl of popcorn that sat on the glass table in the middle of Lila Fowler's enormous den.

"Me too," Grace Oliver agreed, throwing a piece of popcorn into the air and catching it in her mouth. "It's my favorite video show."

"Quick. It's Melody Power! Turn up the sound— I love this song," Kimberly Haver said.

Lila reached for the remote and turned up the sound of the huge, wide-screen TV. Pounding rock-and-roll music began to pour through the stereo speakers that were arranged all around the room.

Twelve-year-old Jessica Wakefield began to move her shoulders to the beat. The Fowlers' sound system was amazing. Nobody else at Sweet Valley

Middle School had a system like Lila's. Jessica felt a familiar twinge of jealousy. Lila was Jessica's best friend, but sometimes it was hard to have a best friend who had absolutely everything.

Lila's father was one of the richest people in Sweet Valley. He and Mrs. Fowler were divorced, and since he felt guilty about Lila not having a mom around, he tried to make it up to her by spoiling her to death.

The result was that the whole Fowler home was like a great big dream come true. The den had a huge TV and a SonicSurround home-theater sound system. There was an Olympic-size pool in the backyard. In Lila's room there was a telephone with three lines, and two walk-in closets bulging with expensive clothes.

Jessica looked around the opulent den, where the members of the Unicorn Club were gathered to watch RockTV, the hippest rock-video show on cable TV.

Tamara was sprawled in a big, leather easy chair. Betsy Gordon was draped over the footstool, her arms within reach of the popcorn bowl. Mary Wallace and Mandy Miller were perched on a cream-colored leather sofa. Grace, Kimberly, and Ellen Riteman lay on their stomachs on the thick carpet.

The Unicorn Club was made up of all the prettiest and most popular girls at Sweet Valley Middle

School. They loved gossip, clothes, boys, and excitement. They were very competitive, which meant they sometimes had trouble getting along. But they all agreed that Melody Power was the best female rock singer in the whole world, and that they would give anything to be a star like her.

The Unicorns were also members of the Booster squad, the Middle School's cheerleaders, so they were very good dancers. Jessica looked around. Everybody was focused on Melody up on the screen dancing across a beautiful tropical beach, and everybody was totally into the music. Grace's feet were tapping, Mary's head was swaying, and Ellen was moving her shoulders.

"Come on," Grace urged, getting up. "These dance steps are pretty easy. Let's try it."

Laughing, Ellen stood next to Grace and they began to execute a little series of kicks and hops.

Tamara jumped up and joined them, watching their feet carefully and doing her best to imitate their steps.

It looked like so much fun, Jessica jumped up too. Her feet were already itching to dance. She hurried over and stood beside Tamara, following the hops and kicks carefully.

"Oops." Jessica started giggling when she accidentally stepped on Tamara's toe.

"Yikes!" Tamara cried as she tried to turn and practically knocked over a lamp.

"Not like that," Lila said quickly. "Here, watch me." She hurried to the center of the room and began to bounce lightly on the balls of her feet, shifting her weight from one side to the other. "See," she said. "It's basically just this step."

"That looks great, Lila," Grace said, mimicking Lila's moves.

One by one, the girls began to get the step.

"Now add the hands," Lila cried over the building volume of the sound system. She waved her hands back and forth as she tossed her head.

Jessica waved her arms along with everybody else, doing her best to look like Lila. She watched Lila's long brown hair sway and her suede-booted feet kick. No doubt about it, Lila had a real flair when it came to dancing.

"OK, follow me," Lila said. She punched the remote control until the sound was up full blast. "Do this with your feet." Lila jumped in the air, crossed and uncrossed her ankles quickly, and came back down. Then she spun around twice and ended up in a semisplit—just like Melody Power.

"All right!" Jessica shouted happily. She jumped in the air and then crossed and uncrossed her ankles, just like Lila. But when she came back down, her feet seemed to get tangled up and she tumbled to the floor.

Boom! She landed heavily on her side.

"Oomph!" she cried as Mary Wallace tried the same move—unsuccessfully—and came down on top of Jessica.

"*Watch out!*" Mary and Jessica shouted together as Janet tripped over her own ankles and came toppling down on them both.

Lila put her hands on her hips and threw back her head with laughter. "You guys are sooooo lame. Here. Watch me do it."

From the floor, Jessica watched Lila's feet as she jumped again, crossed and uncrossed her ankles, spun around, and came down in a semisplit. Her hair gracefully circled her face as she tossed her head back and forth in time to the music.

"*Love you, baby, love you, baby, ohhhhh,*" Melody Power sang. Lila shimmied her shoulders and began moving her lips, mouthing the words along with Melody Power. "*Love you, baby, love you, baby, ohhhhhhh.*"

"Come on, try it!" Lila shouted. "Come on! Here comes the good part."

The entire group scrambled up as the drums began to roll and the last part of the song began to crank up.

"*Love you, baby, love you, baby, love you, baby.*" Melody Power's voice was belting out the lyrics.

Jessica jumped to her feet, determined to get the move right. She tried it again, and this time it felt pretty good.

Grace fell into step beside Jessica. "That's it, Jessica! You're getting it."

"You're getting it too." Jessica grinned, watching Grace spin on the balls of her feet.

"How do you know how to do this?" Tamara asked Lila breathlessly between dance steps.

"Because I've been watching all the videos on the big-screen TV," Lila answered. "I tape them, then I watch them in slow motion. It makes it easier to study their feet and figure out the steps."

"You're so lucky to have this," Grace panted.

"I know," Lila said modestly.

Jessica rolled her eyes.

"Come on, you guys! Let's travel," Lila ordered. She pranced through the den into the living room, leading the rest of the Unicorns in a long line.

The music pounded through the house. Jessica caught a glimpse of the dancing line as it passed by the large mirrored wall in the hallway.

"Kick, two, three, four!" Lila shouted.

The Unicorns kicked their legs in unison.

"*Jump*, two, three, four!" Lila shouted, leading the group in a leaping, kicking move.

"Jump, two, three, four!" The Unicorns echoed her move.

"Spin, bend, jump, and turn!" Lila ordered.

Jessica watched as Lila tossed her head again and her long dark hair went flying around her face like Melody Power's. Jessica tossed her own head, and watched her own long blond hair in the mirror. She saw Grace and Tamara execute another spin in perfect synchronization. *We look great dancing together,* she thought. *Just like a video.*

A VIDEO!

Suddenly she had a great, fabulous, wonderful, incredibly brilliant idea.

"It's the most totally cool idea I've ever heard," Betsy squealed.

"Excellent suggestion," Janet said approvingly.

"Do you really think we could?" Mary breathed.

"Sure," Jessica said. "Any school in this part of California is eligible to enter the RockTV School Days competition. But we'll have to hurry. The deadline is next Friday. And the winner is announced next Saturday."

The girls were all tired, sweaty, and out of breath after dancing and lip-syncing to four Melody Power videos in a row. Now they were sitting in the Fowlers' large kitchen, eating pints of Ken and Harry's chocolate-chip brownie peanut-butter marshmallow ice cream.

One of the best things about watching TV at Lila's was the food. The Fowlers bought ice cream for their huge restaurant-size freezer by the crate. Jessica sat at the table with her very own pint and a spoon.

"Would somebody please tell me what you guys

are talking about?" Tamara said. "We don't get cable. I don't even know what contest that is."

Jessica opened her mouth to explain, but Janet immediately jumped in. "The School Days competition is for amateur video makers. People shoot their own videos—with singing and dancing and costumes and all that. If you win, the station awards your school a complete audio-video system—a big-screen television and multiple speakers."

"How cool!" Tamara exclaimed.

"It would be really great if we could win," Jessica added. "Elizabeth said the VCR in the science room broke last week, and the school doesn't have the budget to replace it right now."

Janet smiled. "Then it's obviously our duty to make a video and try to win that system for the school."

"Right," Jessica said with a giggle. She sat up straighter in her seat, feeling proud of her fellow Unicorns. She couldn't wait to tell Elizabeth about this. Elizabeth thought the Unicorns were shallow and selfish. Jessica knew that Elizabeth sometimes called them "the snob squad." But now they'd be doing something that wasn't snobby or selfish at all. They'd be doing something for the good of the school.

Elizabeth was Jessica's identical twin sister. Both girls were in the sixth grade, and had the same long blond hair and blue-green eyes. They even had the same dimple in their left cheeks. But when it came to personality, Elizabeth and Jessica were completely different people.

Jessica loved being a member of the Unicorns, being part of the in-crowd, being in the middle of things. Elizabeth wasn't interested in that stuff at all. She was a serious student, and she loved to read and write. In fact, she was the editor in chief of the *Sixers*, the official sixth-grade newspaper of Sweet Valley Middle School.

"But how could we make a video?" Betsy asked, interrupting Jessica's thoughts. She scraped the bottom of the pint she was sharing with Kimberly.

"I have a video camera," Lila answered quickly. "We could ask Randy Mason to be our cameraman."

"I don't know," Tamara said doubtfully. "Randy may be the president of the sixth grade, but he's kind of a dork."

"But he knows a lot about video," Betsy argued. "I saw a short film he shot for his social-studies project. It looked really professional."

"We definitely want our video to look professional," Grace agreed.

"Lila already looks professional," Mary pointed out. "She looks like a rock star."

Jessica bit her lower lip in irritation. *Who wouldn't look like a rock star in that outfit?* she thought enviously. Sure, Lila had the dance steps and the rhythm, but she also had a pair of brown leather pants, a washed-silk shirt, and boots that probably cost more than Jessica's entire wardrobe.

"I'll be the director," Janet said quickly. She sounded as though she was commanding more than volunteering. But then again, Janet was an eighth-grader *and* the president of the Unicorns. She reached for a notebook and pencil that lay on the kitchen table and began to make notes. "The Unicorns will be the principal performers. But we might need some extra singers. And we'll need musicians, too."

"Bruce Patman could play lead guitar," Tamara said.

Bruce Patman was a very good-looking seventh-grader. He was kind of conceited and a little stuck on himself, but he had been taking guitar lessons for a long time.

"My brother's been teaching me bass guitar," Betsy volunteered. "And Maria Slater knows how to play keyboards. So let's ask her to be in it."

"Scott Joslin is a drummer. Do you think he'll want to be in the video?" Mary asked.

Janet lifted her eyebrows. "*Everybody* will want to be in the video when they find out that it's a Unicorn production. Don't forget, we *are* the most popular girls at school. But I don't think we should let just anybody be in it."

"I know what you mean," Ellen agreed. "We don't want any dorks in our video making us look uncool."

"Right," Lila said. She smiled. "Just think how great I—I mean, *we*—are going to look on camera."

Jessica narrowed her eyes. *Typical Lila.* It was pretty clear she was already thinking of this as *her* video—even though it had been Jessica's idea.

"I mean, none of has pimples or *braces* or anything like that," Lila added.

Suddenly Janet began to choke on her ice cream.

"Janet!" Mary cried. "Are you OK?"

Jessica reached out along with Grace and Mandy and began slapping Janet on the back.

"I'm fine. I'm fine," Janet insisted. She coughed one last time, then turned her attention back to the notebook. "I, uh, just realized that I may not be able to attend all the rehearsals, so I'm going to appoint Grace to be my assistant director."

"Gee," Grace said in surprise. "That's great. But where are you going to be?"

"Oh, I just may have a few appointments," Janet said vaguely. "Now, let's get back to planning—" She looked around at all the excited faces. "—'Unicorn Rock'."

Two

"I really appreciate your taking over the paper for a couple of days while I get over this cold," Elizabeth Wakefield said to her best friend, Amy Sutton. "But don't you think you're getting a little carried away with this investigative journalism stuff?" she added with a laugh.

"Are you kidding?" Amy exclaimed. Her eyes sparkled with excitement. "If you'd read this book by Carl Birnbaum, you'd be totally into investigative journalism too." She handed Elizabeth a thick book.

"*All the Emperor's Tailors*," Elizabeth read, sitting back in her bed. On the back was a picture of Carl Birnbaum, the famous investigative reporter. He looked like a hard-boiled journalist. His lip was lifted in sort of a snarl.

"It's an incredible story," Amy said. "When he was working for the newspaper in Washington, he found out about some people in the government who were doing dishonest things, like stealing money from public programs. Somebody inside the government leaked the information to him and sent him copies of classified files to prove that it was true. Then he wrote a series of big exposés in the newspaper."

Elizabeth's eyes were wide with interest. "Really?"

Amy nodded. "The crooks tried to stop him by threatening to put him in jail because he had the classified files."

"Wow!"

"But that didn't stop him. He was determined to end the corruption, so he just kept on investigating, kept asking questions, kept his eyes open. Eventually he got all the facts that sent the dishonest people to jail," Amy finished with a satisfied nod. "And Carl Birnbaum wound up winning all kinds of journalism prizes for what he did. Now he's rich and famous."

"Sounds like an incredible story," Elizabeth agreed.

"It is," Amy said. "You know, being an investigative reporter would be so cool. It's like being a detective *and* a reporter. Now I know for sure what I want to be when I grow up," Amy said proudly. "An investigative reporter like Carl Birnbaum." She stood up and posed as if she were on the cover of a book, lifting her lip in a snarl. "Amy Sutton, investigative reporter for the *Sixers*. Exposing scandal and corruption in our community—and our school."

Elizabeth laughed. "Unfortunately, I don't think there's much scandal or corruption at Sweet Valley Middle School."

Amy leaned forward and dropped her voice to a conspiratorial whisper. "You might be surprised. I may have stumbled onto some corruption already."

Elizabeth eagerly sat forward. "Really?"

Amy nodded. "Mrs. Wyler gave Randy Mason ten dollars out of the sixth-grade Student Activities Fund to buy a bulletin board for the student-government meeting room."

"So?"

"So . . . yesterday at the student-government meeting, I was there when Randy brought the bulletin board. He put the change and the receipt on Mrs. Wyler's desk."

Amy dropped her voice even lower. "When nobody was looking, I peeked at the receipt. The bulletin board cost $7.25. Randy left two dollars on the desk." She lifted one eyebrow. "That left seventy-five cents unaccounted for."

Elizabeth laughed. "Randy probably just miscounted."

"Randy Mason would never miscount change. He's one of the biggest brains at school. Straight A's in math."

"You don't mean you think he *stole* seventy-five cents," Elizabeth protested. "Amy! That's a terrible thing to think. Did you ask him about it?"

"I sure did. And you know what he said? He said he'd bought some pushpins at another store. *See?*"

"No. See what?" Elizabeth said blankly. "Why shouldn't he buy pushpins if he bought a bulletin board?"

"Because he didn't have the student government's *authorization* to buy pushpins. It was an unauthorized use of government funds," Amy said firmly.

"AMY!" Elizabeth exclaimed. "That's the dumbest thing I ever heard. What's the big deal if he bought pushpins? That's not a story. That's just Randy using common sense."

Amy's face fell. "I was afraid you were going to say that. Darn! How am I ever going to become a famous investigative reporter if I can't find any real scandal?"

Elizabeth laughed again. "Well, you have to be careful that you don't print things you're not sure about. The paper will get into real trouble if we do. I learned my lesson about that a couple of weeks ago, and . . . and . . . and . . ." Elizabeth's nose wiggled and itched. "Ahhh-choo!"

Amy quickly handed her a tissue from the nearby box. "Geez. That's the fourth time you've sneezed since I got here. I don't think you're over your cold."

"I don't think I am either," Elizabeth admitted. "Every time I think I'm over it, it starts to come back."

"Did I hear a sneeze?" Mrs. Wakefield asked from the hallway.

"Yeah, unfortunately," Elizabeth answered stuffily.

Both Mr. and Mrs. Wakefield appeared at the door of Elizabeth's room.

Amy smiled. "Hi, Mr. Wakefield. Hi, Mrs. Wakefield."

"Hello, Amy," Mr. Wakefield said. "Are we interrupting an editorial meeting?" He spotted the book in Amy's hands. "I read that," he said. "Fascinating stuff."

"I know. I want to write an exposé for the *Sixers*," Amy said. "If I get into trouble like Carl Birnbaum and I need a lawyer, can I call you?"

"Sure," Mr. Wakefield said with a laugh.

Mrs. Wakefield went over and closed the window. "No wonder you're sneezing. It's cold in here."

"Is it?" Elizabeth said in a puzzled voice. "It feels hot to me."

"Uh-oh," Mr. Wakefield said. "I have a feeling Elizabeth is going to miss more school."

"Dad," Elizabeth protested. "I feel fine."

"We'll see how you feel later," Mrs. Wakefield said. "Don't work too hard, girls."

Two seconds after Mr. and Mrs. Wakefield left the room, the door opened again with a loud bang.

Both girls jumped as Jessica came hurtling into the room like a purple whirlwind. As Elizabeth and Amy watched in amazement, Jessica jumped in the air, crossed and uncrossed her ankles, then came down on the balls of her feet, spun around, and landed in a semisplit.

Elizabeth and Amy both burst into applause. "That's great, Jess," Elizabeth said. "You look just like Melody Power. How did you learn to do that?"

"Lila showed me and all the other Unicorns. She'll show you, too. Wait till you guys hear what we're planning."

Elizabeth and Amy both listened eagerly as Jessica filled them in on the video project.

"We're going to call it 'Unicorn Rock'," Jessica finished breathlessly.

"But we're not Unicorns," Elizabeth pointed out.

"We're going to ask certain, selected non-Unicorns to be in it," Jessica answered. "I suggested both of you, and everybody agreed to let you be in it."

Amy rolled her eyes. "Thanks, but no thanks. Except for the Boosters, I stay away from all Unicorn activities."

"Why don't you cover it for the *Sixers*?" Elizabeth suggested. "You won't uncover any scandals, but it will make a interesting story."

"Will you be in it?" Jessica asked Elizabeth.

Elizabeth shook her head and pointed to her desk. "I missed three days of school last week because of this cold, and I've got a lot of homework to catch up on. I really won't have time. That's why Amy is taking over the *Sixers* for me until I get caught up."

"Gee, Lizzie, that's too bad. But I'm glad the *Sixers* is going to be covering it. We're having our first meeting tomorrow afternoon."

"Off the record, Jessica, any chance there's a scandal brewing?" Amy asked hopefully.

"The only scandal brewing is that I'm pretty sure Lila Fowler is going to try to be the star," Jessica answered darkly. "And that *would* be a scandal, considering the whole thing was my idea."

Three

"Wow, Lila. The food's awesome." Tamara took another bite out of a giant chocolate-chip cookie.

It was Monday afternoon, and the entire cast of "Unicorn Rock" was gathered in Lila's garage.

"Yeah," Randy Mason agreed, reaching for a cupcake. "And you did a great job turning this place into a rehearsal studio. Thanks."

"You're welcome," Lila said with a smile. She cast a satisfied eye over the table that she'd had the chauffeur set up in the garage. On it there were sodas, chips, cookies, cupcakes, and lots of other great snacks. She'd told their housekeeper, Mrs. Pervis, to put out food for about twenty people.

She'd also asked Mrs. Pervis to set up a couple of clothes racks in the corner. Then Lila had brought armloads of clothes from her closet to the garage for the "costume department." She didn't particularly like lending her own things, but it was important for everybody in the video to look really good.

Lila had gone to lots of trouble, but there was a good reason: She was determined to keep Jessica Wakefield from taking over this video project completely.

Even though Jessica was her best friend, Lila hated the way Jessica was always trying to compete with her. Jessica never missed an opportunity to show her up or make her look bad. And it seemed as if Jessica had been doing that a lot lately.

Lila's mouth tightened as she watched Jessica argue with Betsy Gordon over who was going to wear a beaded vest. The video project may have been Jessica's idea, but she never would have thought of it if it hadn't been for Lila and her dancing.

It had been Lila who had figured out how to do the complicated steps. It had been Lila who had shown the other girls how do to them. And even though some of them had gotten really good at it, Lila was the one who stood out from the rest of the group.

She tossed her head, practicing the Melody Power "attitude." None of the other girls could pull it off like Lila could, she just knew it. She also knew that if they were going to turn in a winning video, it was going to have to star Lila Fowler—and *not* Jessica Wakefield.

"This stuff is great!" Maria Slater yelled, pulling an Indian-print skirt from the rack and holding it up to her waist.

"Here!" Mandy Miller pulled a sequined baseball cap from a pile of hats. "Put this with it."

"Any stuff for guys in there?" Bruce Patman asked.

"I called the Sunshine House this morning," Lila said. "I ordered six funky print shirts in different boys' sizes. They're in that box over there."

"Wow!" Bruce whistled, heading over to the box with Scott Joslin. "These are awesome."

"Is this everybody?" Randy asked, looking around the garage.

Lila looked around too. Aside from the Unicorns, there was Maria, Brooke Dennis, Amy Sutton with her reporter's notebook, Anna Reynolds who had agreed to help with choreography, and Melissa McCormick. Not to mention the boys. All together, about twenty kids.

"I think so," Lila replied.

"Then don't you think we should get started?" Randy asked.

"Thanks, Randy. I'll take over from here," Janet Howell said in her bossiest voice. Janet was wearing a baseball cap, a bomber jacket, and a whistle around her neck. In her hands were a clipboard and a pen. Obviously, she was taking her role as director very seriously. "Attention, everybody! Attention!" Her voice echoed through the garage, and the group fell silent. "Thank you all for coming," Janet said. "I know we're all looking forward to working together over the next few days on this project."

There was a burst of applause.

"Today, we will assign roles, decide who sings, who dances, who does makeup, wardrobe, etc."

Lots of heads nodded, and Lila looked down at her short leather skirt. She knew which role she wanted. She glanced at Jessica and noticed that Jessica was watching her through narrow eyes.

"Now," Janet said, "will all the musicians please raise their hands?"

Bruce, Maria, Scott, and Betsy all raised their hands.

Janet quickly wrote down their names. "Great. That part's settled. By the way, people, we'll be rehearsing here in Lila's garage. But we'll shoot the actual video on the stage of the school auditorium. Mr. Clark has already given us permission."

There was another burst of applause.

"Just out of curiosity, who's going to be singing lead?" Bruce asked, flipping his long bangs back and fooling with the strings of his metallic-blue electric guitar.

"Me," Lila and Jessica said at exactly the same time.

"You!" Both girls turned to each other in outrage.

Bruce and several of the other kids began to laugh. "Here they go again," Bruce said. "Don't you two ever stop competing?"

"Shut up, Bruce," Lila and Jessica said at the same time.

Lila put her hands on her hips and glared at Jessica. "Give me one good reason why you should be the lead singer."

"I've sung with a band before," Jessica retorted. "What makes you think *you* should be the singer?"

"Excuse me," Janet interrupted in a sarcastic voice. "But since *I'm* the director, it's *my* job to pick the lead singer." She turned to Lila. "What makes you think you should be the lead singer?"

"Didn't I just say that?" Jessica muttered under her breath.

"I have the most stage presence," Lila declared.

"She has the best wardrobe, too," Grace Oliver added.

"She dances as well as Melody Power," Tamara pointed out.

"She looks a lot like Melody Power too," Mary Wallace said thoughtfully.

Lila smiled at the girls who were supporting her. It was nice to hear them saying such complimentary things. She did look like Melody Power. At night, when she danced around her room and lip-synced to her Melody Power CDs, she felt just as professional as Melody Power.

"That doesn't mean she can sing like Melody Power," Jessica argued.

"That's a good point," Mary said.

Several heads nodded, and Jessica gave Lila a little smirk.

Suddenly Lila felt absolutely furious. This time she was going to wipe that smirk off of Jessica's face for good. "For your information," Lila said hotly, "I happen to have a beautiful singing voice."

"You do?" several of the Unicorns asked.

"I do," Lila insisted.

Several eyebrows lifted in surprise.

The skeptical looks irritated her. OK, so maybe she'd never really done any singing. How hard could it be? It sure looked easy when Melody Power did it.

"I know," Randy said, taking another cupcake from the table. "Maybe Jessica and Lila should *audition* for role of lead singer."

Lila sucked in her breath with an insulted gasp. *Audition!* That did it. Talk about nerve. Lila wanted to snatch the cupcake out of Randy's hand and smash it into his face. How dare he? How dare all of them? Here they were in *her* garage, eating *her* food, wearing *her* clothes. How dare they ask her to audition? What a bunch of ingrates!

"A talent like me doesn't audition," she said

coldly. "And besides," she added in a steely voice, "it's *my* video camera."

There was a long silence as everyone digested the significance of her last remark.

Jessica looked furious, but no one said a word.

"Lila Fowler, lead singer," Janet said finally, writing it down on her clipboard.

"OK," Bruce said. "Now that that's settled, what song?"

"How about a Melody Power song?" Tamara suggested.

"How about an original song?" Betsy said.

Immediately everybody began to applaud.

"An original song would probably double our chances of winning the contest," Bruce said. "That would really impress the judges."

"But where are we going to get an original song?" Tamara asked.

"We'll have to write one," Grace answered.

"Who would like to volunteer to write a song?" Janet asked.

No one raised their hand.

"I could write some words," Jessica offered. "Unless Lila wants to do that, too," she added bitterly.

"Jessica Wakefield, lyrics," Janet said as she wrote on her clipboard.

"But what about a tune?" Bruce said. "A song has to have a tune."

"Can't you write the tune?" Jessica said.

"I'm a musician, but I'm not a composer."

"Is anybody at school a composer?" Janet asked with a frown.

"Julie Porter's sister, Johanna, writes songs," Amy said from the back of the group.

"You mean that redheaded girl in the seventh grade who never opens her mouth?" Tamara asked.

There was a long silence.

Janet clapped her hands. "Would you all excuse us, please? The executive production committee needs to hold a quick conference."

Janet motioned to the other Unicorns to gather around. They all put their arms together and formed a huddle.

"She's a dork," Ellen Riteman whispered. "If we have somebody like that in our video, we'll lose the contest."

"Ellen, it's not like she'd be on camera," Janet hissed.

"I've heard she's a really talented musician," Mary said.

"I say we ask her to do it," Janet said.

"What if she won't?"

"Are you kidding?" Tamara cried. "She's a total reject. She'll be honored to be asked to do it."

"I'll ask her personally," Lila offered. "After all, who can say no to a Unicorn?"

Four

"No, thank you," Johanna Porter said, her voice just above a whisper.

Lila's mouth fell open in shock. Was Johanna crazy? Didn't she know what an honor it was to be asked to participate in a Unicorn project? "Why not?" she demanded. "All the coolest and most popular kids are going to be involved."

"That's just it," Johanna said in a soft, quavery whisper. "I don't think I'd really feel comfortable in that group."

Lila frowned. Was Johanna totally weird or something? What kind of person didn't want to do things with the in-crowd?

Johanna hugged her books to her chest and began to walk away.

"Wait!" Lila cried, hurrying after her.

Johanna stopped and turned around.

Lila bit her lip. This wasn't going the way she had expected. She had thought Johanna would jump at the chance, that she'd be incredibly flattered that Lila was paying attention to her, that she'd want to do anything she could to be part of the project.

But Johanna didn't seem interested at all. Lila forced her mouth into a friendly smile. "It's for a good cause."

"It is?"

"Didn't I tell you? The video is going to be entered in a contest on RockTV. We're trying to win an audio-video system for the science room."

"Gosh," Johanna said. "That's great."

"Please say you'll do it," Lila begged, giving Johanna her most charming "let's be buddies" smile. "I think it would be a great opportunity for the two of us to get to know each other better—and I'm so interested in music."

"You are?" Johanna said, her face beginning to relent a little. "I didn't realize that."

"Oh, definitely," Lila said. "I'm totally into music. All the Unicorns are." She studied Johanna's face. It looked a bit wary. Lila decided a little flattery couldn't hurt. "We're all really excited to work with you. We've heard how talented you are."

"Gee," Johanna said, a faint smile lighting up her face. "I had no idea."

"So will you do it?"

Johanna's face closed up a little. "I don't know," she began uncertainly. "I don't really know any of the Unicorns very well."

"But I'll be there," Lila said. "And now you know me. We're having a production meeting this afternoon in my garage. Please say you'll do it. *Please*," she wheedled in her sweetest voice. "We're all so interested in getting to know you better."

Johanna chewed on her lip thoughtfully. "OK," she said. "I'll do it."

"Great! Janet Howell's got everything really well organized. We'll start at three thirty, and it'll go like clockwork."

"OK." Johanna nodded. "I'll see you then."

"Great!" Lila forced her voice into an upbeat, positive tone. But inside, she was feeling angry. *Good grief*, she thought irritably. *I never thought I'd see the day when a Unicorn would have to practically beg a dork like Johanna Porter to come over to her house after school.* Who did Johanna think she was, anyway?

"Elizabeth!" Jessica cried. "Where are you going?"

It was just after third period, and Elizabeth was trudging toward the front door of the school. She looked awful. Her face was white, her eyes were red, and her lips looked cracked.

"I don't feel well," Elizabeth croaked. "I went to

the nurse, and she took my temperature and called Mom. She's coming to pick me up."

"What's the matter?" Jessica asked. "Is your cold back?"

Elizabeth nodded. "Yes. But it's not a cold. It's the flu."

"You idiot!" Tamara shouted. "Get off my foot! That's the third time you've stepped on my foot today!"

"I can't help it!" Grace shouted back. "It's huge! No matter where I step, your big old foot is in my way!"

Johanna took a step farther back into the corner and felt her shoulders hunch involuntarily. Her shoulders always did that when she felt shy and ill at ease. It was almost as if she was trying to disappear.

She'd been in Lila's garage for only ten minutes, and she was already regretting that she'd come. She almost felt like hiding behind the big white Rolls Royce that was parked on the far side of the garage.

Lila had said this was going to be fun and that it would run smoothly. But the kids who were gathered in Lila's garage seemed bossy, disorganized, and mean.

Why did I ever agree to do this? Johanna thought miserably. Just as she expected, she felt shy, awkward, out of place, and geeky.

Skriiieeekkk! went Bruce Patman's electric guitar as he fooled around with one of the knobs.

There was a horrible racket as Scott Joslin tried a few riffs on the snare drum.

Waaa waaaa waaaa went an out-of-tune bass guitar, played by Betsy Gordon.

Over by the musicians, Tamara, Mary, and Grace tried another dance step.

"I told you to watch it!" Tamara shouted again as Mary and Grace both stepped on her toes.

Janet Howell clapped her hands authoritatively. "Try it again, and quit shouting at each other!" she shouted irritably.

The three girls took their positions, and Mary began the count. "One, two, three, and . . ."

On the count of four, Mary jumped to the right just as Grace and Tamara jumped to the left.

"Ouch!" Mary shrieked as she slammed into Grace, who slammed right into Tamara, who went tumbling to the side and . . .

CRASH!

. . . fell right into the drums.

"Hey!" Scott yelled in surprise. He quickly reached out to steady the snare. As he did, he overshot the distance with his arm and went tumbling off his drummer's stool.

He hit the floor and knocked over the bass drum.

The bass drum boomed as it rolled across the floor and . . .

. . . hit Betsy on the backs of her knees, causing her legs to crumple.

Wahhhhhh! went the bass guitar as she dropped it on the floor.

The garage echoed with shouts and shrieks and complaints. Johanna put her hand over her ears. This was a disaster. Quickly she gathered up her purse and book bag. *I'm getting out of here,* she decided. *I don't care what Lila Fowler says.*

Just as she was about to slip under the garage door, the pretty black girl who had been fiddling with the keyboard caught her sleeve. "Hi," she said with a smile. "I've been meaning to introduce myself. I've seen you at school, but we haven't met. I'm Maria Slater."

"Hi," Johanna managed to croak. She could feel her cheeks turning bright pink. Why did that always have to happen whenever she met somebody new?

"Elizabeth says you're a composer," Maria said.

"Um, yeah," Johanna said. She racked her brains for something else to say, but she couldn't think of anything. Why did she always have to be so tongue-tied?

But Maria didn't seem to mind. She looked around the garage and giggled at the knot of arguing kids. "Well, I'd say so far we're right on schedule."

Johanna frowned in confusion.

"Every production I've ever been involved in goes through this phase. Nobody knows what they're doing. Everybody wants to give orders. Nobody wants to take them."

Johanna looked up. "You sound like you've had a lot of experience."

Maria nodded. "Yeah. I was on a couple of TV shows, some feature films, and a lot of commercials when I was younger."

Johanna studied Maria's face and gasped. "You do look really familiar. Were you in *Mansion of Blood*?"

"That was me." Maria laughed. "The life of a child actor can be pretty bizarre," she explained with a grin, "so my parents took me out of show business for a while. We left Los Angeles and came here so I could get a good junior high and high school education. How about you?" Maria asked. "Your family is in the music business, right? Have you had any professional experience?"

"My dad is a violinist and conductor. My mom is a concert pianist. And my sister plays the flute," Johanna said in a soft voice. "But I'm more a behind-the-scenes kind of person." Her eyes dropped to her feet. Maria was getting into a sore subject. Everybody in Johanna's whole family was good at performing. Her mom got up and played the piano in front of thousands of people. Her dad never missed an opportunity to perform—professionally or at parties. Even her own little sister, Julie, played the flute in the California Gifted Students' Orchestra. In fact, she was rehearsing every afternoon and evening these days for an upcoming performance.

Everybody in her family was always urging her to perform the songs she wrote. But just the thought of it made Johanna sick to her stomach. She wished with all her might that she could somehow work up the nerve to get up in front of people and sing her songs. Every night when Johanna sat down at her piano to work on her songs, she fantasized about being a professional singer and songwriter. She loved to sing and play the piano, pretending that people were watching her.

But pretending was one thing. Actually performing was something else. Shy people weren't good performers. Good performers were extroverted, outgoing, and always at ease, like Maria or like Julie. Just thinking about actually singing on a stage made Johanna feel queasy and kind of dizzy.

Johanna swallowed the big lump in her throat and pushed the mental picture of herself onstage to the back of her mind. Then Johanna felt an insistent tug at her sleeve. "Johanna," Jessica interrupted. "I just finished these lyrics. What do you think?"

Johanna took the sheet of paper from Jessica, grateful to have the subject changed. Now they were getting into something she enjoyed—songwriting.

"Well," she said, "all this looks pretty good."

"Really?" Jessica exclaimed. "You like the part about math blues?"

"Yeah. I think it's cute the way you rhymed Arnette with hairnet. It's not what's called a perfect rhyme, but it's close enough."

Jessica smiled at Maria. "The song's about a girl who falls in love with a guy in her math class," she explained.

Johanna studied the page, mentally setting the words to a rhythm. "I think you've got one too many A sections, so let's cut this section here. The usual way to construct a rock song is A A B A."

Jessica was peering over Johanna's shoulder with great interest. Bruce and Betsy had come over to listen too.

"This is pretty exciting," Betsy said. "I've never seen a composer at work before."

Johanna drew her pencil through one of the lines at the bottom. "And this doesn't really rhyme here. Oops," she cried as the tip of her pencil broke. She looked around. "I need a pen or a pencil," she said. "Does anybody have one?"

"Here, take mine." A hand reached forward with a very expensive-looking pen. Lila gave Johanna a dazzling smile. "I'm really glad you're writing my song," she said.

"Your song?" Johanna said in confusion. "I didn't realize you were the singer."

"The *lead* singer," Lila confirmed.

"Even though she doesn't know anything about music," Jessica muttered sourly.

"Lila knows a lot about music," Betsy protested.

"That's right," Bruce said. "She said she knew more about music than all of us put together."

All of a sudden, Johanna began to feel better. These kids were nicer than she thought. And if Lila knew a lot about music, this project might really turn out to be fun. "What's your key, so I know what to put the tune in," Johanna asked.

Lila's face took on a funny look. "Oh, any old key will be fine."

"But . . ."

"I'm sure anything you write will be just great," Lila said happily. "You're such great composer."

Johanna wished Lila could be a little more specific. But she decided not to ask again. After all, she'd always heard her parents say that great singers were eccentric.

Five

"OK," Janet shouted on Wednesday afternoon. "You all have your music. Let's get ready for a run-through."

Johanna sat on the hood of the Rolls Royce and watched eagerly as the musicians peered at their sheet music, positioning their fingers to play.

"This tune is fantastic," Maria said, humming it as she sight-read the music and played it on the electric keyboard.

"I love the chord progression," Bruce commented, sliding his fingers up and down the neck of the guitar.

"But we can't all read the music," Grace said to Maria.

Maria plinked a couple of the keys on the piano. "Don't worry. All you have to do is follow Lila. The background vocals are just a repetition of the main melody lines. When she sings, just repeat the line softly behind her."

"Come on, Jessica!" Janet commanded. "Get with the background singers and get ready to follow Lila."

"Let's do it," Randy said, hoisting the video camera onto his shoulder. "Everybody get ready for a practice take."

Lila stepped up to the microphone.

Bruce began the count. "One and two and three . . ."

A chill ran up Johanna's spine as Bruce played the intro chords. They were soft and romantic.

Boom boom boom te boom! came the drums, picking up the tempo and giving the song a slight rock-and-roll beat.

Betsy's fingers began to pluck at the strings of her bass guitar, and Maria bent over the keyboard and began to fill in the melody.

"Ohhhhhhh, babyyyyyy," sang the background singers.

Johanna's breath caught heavily in her throat. She'd never heard a band play one of her songs before. Now that it was actually being played, it sounded better than she had ever dreamed.

It wasn't actually a new melody—it was one that she'd been working on for a while. It was one of the best she had ever written. As soon as she had seen Jessica's lyrics, she had gone home and tried singing them to her tune. The words had fit almost perfectly. Johanna had just had to make a few minor rhythm adjustments to make the words go with the music.

Even though it was a first run-through and the musicians were a little rough, the beautiful melody was clear as a bell. She'd written the music out as simply as possible so that it would be easy to play. The result was that even on the first try, the band sounded almost professional.

Lila looked just like a professional singer, too. She was wearing a leather fringed skirt, suede boots, a denim shirt, and a wide silver belt.

Johanna couldn't wait to hear Lila sing.

Lila's shoulders began to sway back and forth to the music.

The long introduction reached its climax and . . .

"I can't read this," Lila said into the mike. "My copy is too light."

Abruptly the music came to an end.

"Geez." Scott sighed in disappointment. "We were just getting going."

"I'm sorry," Lila sniffed. "But I can't sing it if I can't even see the notes on the page."

"I have another copy," Johanna said quickly. Her cheeks were flushing scarlet as she fished around in her book bag and located another copy. How could she have been so dumb? She should have made sure Lila's copy was nice and bold.

"Sorry," she muttered as she handed the new copy to Lila.

"OK then," Bruce shouted. "Let's do it from the top. One! Two! Three!"

The opening chords echoed through the garage, the drums and the bass and the electric piano all blending beautifully.

Lila tossed her long mane of dark hair and stepped up to the mike. She threw back her head, opened her mouth, and then immediately spoke into the microphone. "It's too cold in here."

Screeecch! went Bruce's electric guitar as he ran his hand over the strings in frustration. "Lila!" he shouted. "Are you going to sing this song or not?"

"I can't sing when it's this cold."

"I have a sweater," Tamara said, hurrying to get it out of her backpack.

She handed it to Lila, who draped it over her shoulders.

"Let's try it again!" Janet shouted. "Everybody take your places."

Johanna sat up straighter. Now, finally, she'd get to hear the song she had written.

Lila held the music up to her face, studying it as the introduction built to a climax.

The drums came in again.

The backup singers began to hum.

Lila tossed her hair back off of her shoulders, opened her mouth, and . . .

. . . frowned again at the page. "My head hurts," she said in a small voice.

"LILA!" the entire cast shouted.

Johanna chewed on her fingernail. Lila sure was acting like a prima donna.

"If your head hurts that badly, maybe I should sing it," Jessica said quickly.

"That does it," Lila said angrily, stamping her foot. "You've just completely blown my concentration, Jessica Wakefield! I can't possibly learn a new song in this atmosphere of hostility."

"Oh, yeah?" Jessica taunted, her eyebrows coming together angrily.

"Yeah!" Lila retorted.

"Look," Maria said calmly. "Lila has a point. I've seen performers choke up before with new material. It even happens to pros. Lila, why don't you and Johanna go into the house and rehearse at the piano in private? The rest of us can keep practicing on our own out here."

"Excellent suggestion," Janet said.

The knot in Johanna's stomach began to loosen up. She'd been getting worried about Lila's ability to sing. But Maria was right. She probably just needed a little time and privacy.

"You can't read music?" Johanna said in surprise.

Lila shook her head. "I never learned how."

"Why didn't you just say so?" Johanna asked.

Lila shrugged. She didn't like admitting that she was wrong or that she didn't know how to do something. It made her feel small and insignificant. And the only way she could make herself feel better was to make somebody else feel smaller. Lila immediately thought of a dozen cutting things she could say to Johanna that would make her feel small.

But when she looked at Johanna's pale face, with its sprinkling of freckles across the nose and her light-blue eyes, she quit worrying about feeling small. Johanna looked as though she already felt pretty small. Lila didn't need to cut her down in order to feel OK.

Besides, Johanna seemed really nice. Not like somebody who would ever be nasty. Not like some of the Unicorns. Not like Jessica. She seemed like somebody it would be safe to confide in.

"Because I was embarrassed," Lila said truthfully. "Most of those other kids seemed like they knew how to read music, and I didn't. I'm the lead singer. I should know how to read music."

Johanna smiled. "Not being able to read music is nothing to be ashamed of," she said. "Don't worry, I can teach you the song."

"I still feel pretty dumb," Lila said, flicking her hair off of her shoulder. "It's hard not to be able to do something everybody else seems to be able to do."

"Tell me about it," Johanna said with a wry smile. "I feel that way all the time."

"You do?"

"Sure. Things that seem simple for everybody else are really hard for me. Things like walking into a room full of people and saying hello. Or not blushing when people talk to me. Making friends. And forget about performing—I'd rather die than perform in front of people."

"Really?" Lila said. "I thought everybody in your family was some kind of musical performer."

"Everybody but me. It's really awful, and it makes my parents furious, but I won't even go to my own piano recitals."

"Why not?" Lila cried. "If you worked hard to learn a piano piece, why wouldn't you want to show off?"

Johanna shook her head. "I just feel nervous and scared when I know people are watching me. I guess it's because I'm shy."

Lila began to giggle. "We're total opposites. Once I get on the stage, you have to have a hook to get me off."

"That's because you're *not* shy," Johanna said. "I wish I were more like you."

"It's all attitude," Lila explained. "You've just got to take the attitude that you're really great. When you walk into a room, hold your head up and say *hi*, like you know how much everybody wants to see you. You can put on a really great outfit, but if you don't wear it with an attitude, nobody will notice. My attitude is, I'm Lila Fowler—the *fabulous* Lila Fowler. I'm great-looking, I've got tons of money, loads of talent, and I'm fabulous. Sometimes I really feel that way, and sometimes I'm just acting like I do."

Lila tossed her head around in an exaggerated parody of a glamorous movie star. Then she giggled. "The only trouble is, sometimes I get a little carried away with my own attitude—like, I wind up pretending to be able to read music when I can't."

Johanna sat down at the piano. "It'll be our secret," she said with a laugh. "Now, let's see some of that famous Fowler talent."

"*I love you sooooooo,*" Lila warbled, holding the last note as long as she could.

It was all Johanna could do not to wince. "You hit the wrong note again," she said as nicely as possible. "The last note is an F sharp, not an F."

"Oh," Lila said. "It sounded OK to me."

Johanna sighed. That last note had sounded like a cat with its tail being pulled. Couldn't Lila even tell? "Let's try it again," Johanna suggested.

"Sure," Lila said, assuming Melody Power's singing stance—arms out, head thrown back, and hip cocked.

"Let's take it from the last line," Johanna said, plinking one of the keys to help Lila find her note. "There," she said, "now go ahead."

"*I love you soooooo . . .*" Lila bellowed at the top of her lungs.

"Good try," Johanna said encouragingly. "But I'm afraid you missed it again."

"You mean I hit an F sharp again?" Lila asked.

"Actually, you hit a B flat."

Lila's face looked blank.

"Listen," Johanna said. "Maybe if you heard the whole song from start to finish, it would give you a better idea of how it's supposed to sound. I'll sing it for you." Johanna spread her fingers over the keys and lightly played the opening bars.

Then she started to sing.

Lila's breath caught in her chest. She couldn't believe it. Dorky little Johanna Porter had the most beautiful singing voice she had ever heard—on or off the radio.

Johanna's eyes closed as she began to sing the last few bars, the ones that Lila had found so difficult. Her voice glided easily over the notes, climbed an octave, and held the last note in a pure, crystal-clear soprano for several moments.

"*Unbelievable!*" Lila shouted as soon as Johanna's voice faded sweetly away. Automatically her hands began to applaud.

Johanna smiled and began to blush. "That's

more or less the way the song is supposed to sound," she said.

"Of course," Lila said. "Now I get it."

"Want to try it again?" Johanna asked.

Lila nodded eagerly. She felt sure that now that she'd heard Johanna sing it properly, she would be able to imitate her voice. Johanna made it sound so easy.

"I love you soooooooo," Lila screeched.

Johanna's heart plummeted down into her shoes. They'd been at it for over two hours. The other kids had gone home long ago, but Lila and Johanna had kept practicing in the privacy of the living room. Johanna had even sung the song into a tape for Lila to sing along with. Lila wasn't getting any better, though. If anything, she was getting worse. And she didn't even seem to be aware of it.

Maybe she was tone-deaf.

"How was that?" Lila asked eagerly.

"Well . . ." Johanna began. She wet her lips, trying hard to think of something encouraging to say.

Fortunately, she didn't have to say anything, because just then Mrs. Pervis knocked softly on the door and stuck her head in. "Johanna," she said, "your mother just called. She says she's expecting you home for dinner in half an hour."

"Thank you," Johanna said. "I'll be ready to go in a minute."

"Well," Lila bubbled happily as Johanna gathered up her things. "I think I've made a lot of progress. What do you think?"

Johanna swallowed. She didn't want to lie. But on the other hand, she didn't want to hurt Lila's feelings.

But Lila didn't wait for an answer. "Oh, there may be a few rough spots, but it's stupid to be discouraged, right? I've just got to practice, practice, practice."

Johanna nervously wet her lips. "That's the attitude," she croaked.

Six

◇

"Where's Julie and Dad?" Johanna asked, sitting down to the dinner table that night.

"Julie is at rehearsal," her mother answered. "And your father is working with a chamber group tonight. He'll pick Julie up on his way home."

"Oh. I sort of need to talk to Julie," Johanna said with a sigh.

Julie Porter was as outgoing and extroverted as Johanna was shy and introverted. But the two girls were very close. They'd hardly had a chance to talk to each other lately, since Julie's orchestra had started preparing for their big annual benefit concert. Julie spent almost every afternoon at rehearsal, and by the time she got home, there was barely enough time to have dinner and get her homework done before she had to go up to her room and practice. These days, it seemed as if the only time Johanna got to talk to Julie was between classes at school.

Johanna looked around the dinner table. As usual, it was beautifully set with salt and pepper shakers from Vienna, plates from Italy, and silver from Mexico. In fact, the Porters' whole house was full of interesting and beautiful things collected by the family on their various tours.

Mrs. Porter traveled to Europe at least once a year to perform. And Mr. Porter had been all over the world with the Sweet Valley Symphony Orchestra.

Johanna reached for the pepper and began to sprinkle it on her salad.

"So, how is your video project going?" Mrs. Porter asked. "Are the kids talented?"

"Well," Johanna hedged. "Some are more talented than others."

"I hope you're singing," her mother said with a smile. "I can't believe that any of them have a voice like yours."

"Mom!" Johanna protested. "I've told you before. I don't want to perform. It's one thing to sing around here with you and Dad and Julie, but singing in front of other people is something else."

"But you have so much talent, Johanna. And people who have talent have a responsibility to share it. People who won't share their talent are like misers who won't share their money."

Johanna smiled. "Speaking of money, the lead singer is Lila Fowler."

"George Fowler's daughter?"

Johanna nodded.

Her mother looked up. "Is she a good singer?"

"She's really nice," Johanna said with a smile. "And I think she wants to be my friend."

"I love you soooooo," Lila warbled in her room that night.

Hmmmmm. That didn't really sound too good. Lila went over to her mirror, bent over, and shook her hair back. There. Now she looked more like Melody Power.

She threw back her head, held out her arms, and took a deep breath. *"I love you soooo!"* she sang at the top of her lungs.

"Owwwwwooooooo," came a faint sound from outside.

"I love you soooooo!" she sang again, trying hard to master that last note.

"Owwwwooooo," came the sound again. Lila cocked her ear. It sounded like the neighbors' dog.

Lila took the biggest, deepest breath that she could, assumed the Melody Power position, and let 'er rip. *"I LOVE YOU SOOOOOOO!"*

"Owwwwoooooooo!" It was the neighbors' dog again.

"Owwwooooo! Owwooooo!" came an answering howl from the other side of the street.

"Yip yip yip!" joined in the terrier that ran loose in the neighborhood.

Lila hurried to the window and shut it with a bang. OK, so maybe she wasn't the greatest singer in the world. But that didn't mean she was going to take criticism from the neighborhood *dogs*.

"I love you sooooo!" Lila trilled in the shower as the water rinsed the suds from her hair. Singing in the shower was fun—the acoustics were great.

"Ohhhhh, baby, I love you sooooo!" she sang even louder, trying to make her voice tremble a little on the last few notes, as Johanna's did.

BAM! BAM! BAM!

Someone was banging on the bathroom door!

"Lila!" she heard her father's voice call. "Are you OK in there?"

Lila stepped out of the shower, threw on her thick terry-cloth robe, and opened the bathroom door.

"What's wrong?" she gasped, noticing the worried look on her father's face.

Mr. Fowler ran a hand over his forehead. "I'm so relieved. I heard that awful noise in there and I thought you were in terrible pain. Are you sure you're all right?"

* * *

"*I love you soooooooo,*" Lila sang in front of the mirror. She looked at her mouth, which was forming a perfect O as she held on to the last, long, liquid note of the song.

The voice that filled the room was high and clear. It sounded perfect, beautiful.

The only trouble was, it was Johanna's voice. On tape.

Lila was lip-syncing.

She went over to her tape player and flipped it off with a sigh. Then she sat down on her bed and groaned. "Who am I kidding?" she wailed out loud. "All the attitude in the world isn't going to make my voice sound good. I'll never be able to sing this song."

She closed her eyes and shuddered, thinking of all the bragging she had done. If she backed out now, or made a fool of herself by trying to sing, she'd never live it down.

"Why did I ever open my big mouth?" she grumbled. Singing along with a Melody Power tape was one thing. But she was finally beginning to realize that being the lead singer—where you had to actually hit *all* the notes of a song—was another.

She climbed under the covers and pulled the blanket over her head. Maybe she should drop out. Say she had a cold or something. Let Jessica sing the song.

She could be incredibly gracious about it. Act as if she was doing Jessica a huge favor. In fact, if she did it right, she could have Jessica being *grateful* to her.

Lila poked her head out from under the blanket and settled herself more comfortably against her pillow. Then she began mentally rehearsing her resignation speech.

"So, how's the video going?" Julie asked Johanna the next morning. The two sisters were standing by their lockers between first and second period. The first bell had already rung, and most of the students had already gone into their second-period classrooms.

Johanna was searching quickly through her locker for her math book. She had only another minute or two before the second bell rang.

"I wish I could be in it," Julie went on, rummaging around inside her own locker. "It sounds like sooooo much fun. But the orchestra is meeting every afternoon this month and I don't have any free time. You are so lucky."

Johanna felt her face fall into a frown.

"Gee, Johanna, you don't exactly look happy about it," Julie said quickly. "Is something wrong?" Her face darkened slightly. "Are the Unicorns being obnoxious to you? Sometimes those girls are so snobby."

Johanna shook her head and darted a look around to make sure nobody could hear her. She dropped her voice to a whisper. "I'm just worried that Lila won't be ready to sing by the day after tomorrow," she said unhappily.

"Really?" Julie whispered. "How come?"

Maria Slater came around the corner then and gave them both a big smile. Johanna smiled back and waited until Maria had disappeared into Mrs. Wyler's classroom. "She's having a little trouble learning the song," she whispered.

"But you showed me a copy of the song," Julie said. "It didn't look difficult. I wonder why she's having a hard time learning it."

"Because . . ." Johanna began. She hated to say it. Lila had tried so hard, and it seemed so important to her to sing. Besides, Johanna was almost beginning to feel as though Lila was her friend. She didn't want to be disloyal. "The second bell's about to ring," she said. "I'll tell you later."

She started to hurry off, but Julie grabbed her sleeve and pulled her back. "Come on, out with it. What's up?" Julie asked in a soft but insistent voice.

"Well." Johanna nervously tapped her foot. "I guess I'm trying to say that Lila can't sing," she confessed miserably.

"I thought she was supposed to be a great singer!" Julie exclaimed.

"Shhhh," Johanna warned, seeing Mandy Miller

throw them a curious look as she came around the corner. "She's not. And it's pretty discouraging. I just don't know what to do. She's never going to be able to sing the song well enough for the video—and I'm worried she'll wind up embarrassing herself."

"Not to mention ruining the song you and Jessica wrote." Julie sighed. "What a mess. But maybe she'll realize that she's not doing so well and let somebody else sing the song."

"That's what I'm hoping," Johanna said. "We're supposed to get together this afternoon. Maybe she'll be ready to throw in the towel after another rehearsal." Johanna crossed her fingers just as the second bell rang.

So Lila can't sing, Jessica thought happily. She was crouched on the other side of the lockers, and she had just overheard the whole whispered conversation between Johanna and Julie.

She peeked around the corner and watched as Julie and Johanna hurried to their classes.

Don't you worry, Jessica thought smugly. *Lila will be ready to throw in the towel by this afternoon. I'm going to make sure of that.*

"What are you doing?" whispered a voice at her elbow.

"Yeowww!" Jessica cried. She was so startled she dropped her books.

Amy Sutton stepped backward. "Wow! I had a feeling you might be up to something, the way you were crouched there. What were you doing? Spying?"

Jessica pursed her lips together. "I was *not* spying," she said huffily.

Amy lifted one eyebrow. "It looked like you were spying to me. And if you *weren't* spying, why do you look so guilty?"

"None of your business," Jessica said firmly. She didn't want to admit that she had been eavesdropping. Sometimes Amy could be just as much of a goody-goody as Elizabeth.

Amy cocked an eyebrow. "I smell a story," she said with a knowing smile.

"Listen, I gotta go," Jessica said quickly. "I'm already late for class." She hurried down the hall before Amy could say another word. She didn't have time to talk to Amy. She was too busy thinking up a good way to psyche Lila into resigning as lead singer.

Lila sat down at the Unicorner with her tray and began to unload the little dishes that held meat loaf, mashed potatoes, and Jell-O. She'd spent all night rehearsing her gracious resignation speech. She was going to say that since Jessica had written the words, "professional courtesy dictated that she let Jessica interpret her own creative work."

She smiled as she removed the apple from her tray. It had taken her over two hours to come up with that phrase, and she was pretty proud of it.

But before she could say anything, Jessica let out a nasty snicker. "I read a really interesting article about the theater," she began, looking directly at Lila. "It said that sometimes, in the old days, if singers were really bad, the people in the audience would throw rotten fruit and vegetables at them."

"You're kidding!" Tamara exclaimed. "How gross."

"Just think how awful it would be for a singer to have that happen," Jessica said, shaking her head at Lila.

Lila took a bite of her meat loaf and chewed slowly, studying Jessica's face. It had that bland, wide-eyed look. Lila knew what that look meant: Jessica was up to something. And it wasn't hard to figure out what. She was trying to psyche Lila out. Trying to scare her out of being the lead singer.

"Today," Jessica continued, "audiences just boo until the singer stops singing and gets off the stage."

"That's so mean," Grace said indignantly.

"It sure is," Jessica agreed. "And just think how horribly embarrassing it would be for the singer. Don't you think so, Lila?" she asked in a sickly-sweet voice.

"Luckily, Lila doesn't have to worry about any-thing like that," Betsy said. Then her brow furrowed. "Do you?" she asked in a doubtful voice.

"Of course not," Lila snapped. "Don't be silly."

"That's good," Jessica said. "Because I heard that practically the entire school is going to be in the auditorium while we shoot. They all want to watch us perform."

"They do?" Lila asked.

Jessica nodded. "And in that article I was reading, it said that at one concert the audience got so mad at the singer because she was so terrible that they pulled all the seats apart." She took a bite of her Jell-O. "Just think how mad Mr. Clark would be at all of us if something like that happened."

There was dead silence as the Unicorns all looked at one another.

"You know," Grace said slowly, "none of us have actually heard you sing, Lila."

Tamara put her fork down. "That's right," she said in a whisper. "We haven't."

Jessica smiled sweetly at Lila. "Gosh. You know, that's true. None of us have ever heard you sing one, solitary note. Are you *sure* you want to be the lead singer?"

Lila dropped her fork on her plate with a loud clatter and gritted her teeth. Up until now, she'd been considering graciously backing out and insisting that Jessica sing the song. But now—now there was no way that she was going to give her the satisfaction.

She stood up and lifted her chin. "I know what you're trying to do, Jessica Wakefield. And it won't work!"

Lila hurried out of the lunchroom, fuming. She was so mad she could hardly see straight. As she passed the art room, she heard the radio playing softly. It was playing one of her favorite Melody Power songs. One of the songs she liked to lip-sync in front of the mirror.

Lila froze.

Suddenly she had an idea. A brilliant, incredible idea. She turned on her heel and hurried toward the auditorium to check the sound set-up.

Seven

"I can't sing the song," Lila announced that afternoon as soon as Johanna took her seat at the piano. "I've practiced and practiced, but I just can't seem to get the hang of it. Somebody else is going to have to sing it."

Johanna's face lit up. "That's great." Then immediately she began to blush. "I mean . . . what a shame. But I'm sure Jessica will do a great job."

"Jessica Wakefield will sing the song over my dead body," Lila responded calmly. She saw Johanna's eyebrows rise in surprise.

"But I thought Jessica was your friend," Johanna said.

Lila studied Johanna's face. It looked open and honest. It looked trusting and sweet. It didn't look like the kind of face that would be involved in anything that wasn't completely on the up-and-up. *Hmmmm,* Lila thought, her mind racing. How was she going to get Johanna to go along with her scheme?

"Jessica isn't anybody's friend," she lied. "Nobody likes Jessica."

"But the other Unicorns all seem . . ."

"That's because Jessica's got them all over a barrel," Lila declared. "Jessica is a *blackmailer*."

Johanna gasped. "What do you mean?"

"Jessica is always doing whatever she can to find out embarrassing secrets about people. Then, if they don't act friendly and do what she wants, she threatens to tell."

Johanna's jaw dropped. "That's awful."

Lila nodded sadly. "I know. And I'm in a terrible situation. Because if Jessica found out I couldn't sing the song after all the bragging I did . . . it's too awful to think about." Lila shook her head. "You probably know that my father is . . . well, pretty well off. I don't know what Jessica would demand to keep quiet about this." She lowered her eyes. "I know it's my own fault," she said tearfully. "I know I shouldn't have bragged about being able to sing, but Jessica was being so mean to me . . . and I really did think I'd be able to do it and . . ." Her voice broke in a sob.

She snuck a peak at Johanna and saw that Johanna was looking very sympathetic. "Don't worry," Johanna said, patting Lila's shoulder. "Don't worry. I'll teach you the song. *Somehow.*"

Lila shook her head. "It's no good. I can't sing it."

"But if you don't sing it, and Jessica doesn't sing it, who will?"

"You," Lila answered.

"*Me!*" Johanna gasped. As Lila watched, her face turned red, then pink, then white. Then it turned red again, and her mouth curved into almost a smile. "Do you think I could?" she whispered in a frightened but hopeful voice. "I've always had a real phobia about performing, but maybe now, with someone like you encouraging me . . ."

"Sure you should sing it," Lila said, forcing her voice to sound sincere. "I mean, it's your song. You'd be great. Just picture it. *You* are the center of attention. Every eye is on *you*. Everyone is listening to *you* sing. Listening to every note *you* are singing."

She noticed Johanna gulp nervously. Lila held up her hands and stared intently at Johanna's face. "The pressure is on," she said in an intense voice. "But do you care?"

"Yes!" Johanna said.

"No!" Lila argued dramatically. She put her hand on Johanna's shoulder and clasped it. "Of course you don't care. Because you're a pro. Sure, you could goof it up and ruin the whole thing . . ."

Johanna gasped.

"Sure, you could have people laughing at you . . ."

Johanna shrank back against the piano.

"Sure, the audience could start throwing rotten fruit and vegetables, and maybe even start pulling the seats apart . . ."

Johanna covered her face and groaned.

"But you won't care about any of that stuff, because deep down, you know you're a major talent."

"No, I don't," Johanna whimpered, looking completely demoralized. "Deep down, I know I'm a major weenie." Her face was white and her voice was shaking.

"Johanna!" Lila protested.

Johanna's fingers trembled as they flew to her cheeks. "I'd rather die than sing the song!" she blurted defiantly.

Lila let her mouth fall open in mock shock and surprise. "What do you mean? You *have* to sing the song. Nobody else can sing it. Not Jessica. Not anybody. Nobody has as good a voice as you do. Don't you want the science department to have the VCR?"

Johanna jumped to her feet and began to gather up her things. "I won't do it," she muttered miserably, stuffing her sheet music into her backpack. "I don't care what you say. I won't do it, and I'm through with this video project."

She headed for the door, practically at a run.

"Wait!" Lila cried. "Johanna, wait!"

Johanna reluctantly stopped, and Lila hurried over to her. "You seem so upset. Please don't rush away like this."

"I can't help it," Johanna choked. "I feel terrible—like I'm letting everybody down. I know the school needs a VCR, but I'm just too scared. I feel awful—about *everything*. My mother is always saying that people with talent have a responsibility to share it. But I don't want the responsibility."

Lila snapped her fingers, as if she had just had a great idea. "Listen," she said. "I may have a way out of this problem that would work for us both." She took Johanna's arm. "Come on and sit down."

When they were seated on the couch in the den and Johanna had calmed down a little, Lila confided to Johanna what she had been planning since lunchtime. But she acted as if she had just thought of it.

"Do you really think it would work?" Johanna asked when Lila had finished.

Lila nodded. "Sure. Why wouldn't it?"

"It doesn't seem, well . . . honest."

"Nobody will even know." Lila smiled. "And besides, your school is counting on you."

"Well, I guess," Johanna said reluctantly. "I guess I could try it."

Lila reached out her hand and clasped Johanna's. "No. *We'll* try it," she said with a smile. "We're in this together."

Johanna's face almost glowed. "Wow. I guess that really does make us . . . *friends.*"

Lila smiled. "I guess it does."

"She's going to blow it," Jessica hissed to Mandy. "I just know she's going to blow it."

Johanna pretended not to hear the conversation as she quietly checked the microphones.

It was Friday, the afternoon of the video shoot, and all the participants were gathered on the stage area of the auditorium. The audience was full of kids who had come to watch. Jessica and Mandy were standing a few feet away from Johanna, just behind the curtain.

"She's going to make herself look bad, she's going to make the Unicorns look bad, and she's going to make Sweet Valley Middle School look bad. I happen to know that Lila Fowler can't sing at all," Jessica whispered to Mandy.

"How do you know that?"

Johanna felt her stomach flip-flop.

"I overheard a conversation between Johanna and Julie," Jessica answered.

Ohhhhh, Johanna thought angrily. So Jessica was an eavesdropper *and* a blackmailer. Up until now, Johanna hadn't felt one hundred percent sure that she was doing the right thing. But now . . . now she was going to *enjoy* making Jessica eat her words.

Johanna continued fiddling with the mikes while straining her ears to listen to the rest of their conversation.

"Where's Elizabeth?" Mandy asked. "How come she's not in the audience?"

"She's still home sick," Jessica said. "She's got the flu. Where's Janet?"

Mandy shrugged. "She said she had an appointment this afternoon. She told Grace to supervise the shoot if she didn't get back in time."

"Must be a pretty important appointment," Jessica exclaimed. "I can't imagine anything important enough to keep Janet away from this today. Besides, she's supposed to sing backup with us."

Mandy shrugged and grinned. "If she doesn't come, you and I will just have to sing louder, that's all."

"Places, everybody!" Grace shouted, clapping her hands and adjusting Janet's baseball cap on her head. "Places. We're getting ready to shoot."

Nervous butterflies filled Johanna's stomach.

She saw the dancers and the singers take their places. Over in the wings, she saw Lila shake out her long brown hair and head toward the mikes.

"I'm here!" she heard a voice call out. Just then she saw Janet taking off her jacket and hurrying over to confer with Grace.

Johanna shot a look around the stage. Satisfied

that no one was watching, she quickly flipped off the sound switch of the microphone Lila would be holding. Then she bent over the amplifier and plugged in another mike.

She looked down at the floor. There were so many wires and cables on the floor of the stage, no one would ever notice the one that led all the way backstage and behind the curtain.

"I love you soooooo," Lila sang, holding the last, sweet, silvery note an impossibly long time.

When the last echo had finally died away, there was a stunned hush . . . and then the audience exploded with applause.

"CUT!" Grace shouted.

"Fantastic!" Randy yelled. "Not one mistake. The first take was absolutely flawless. It's a wrap."

Jessica couldn't believe it. It was the most unbelievable thing she had ever heard in her life. If Lila's voice was so bad, how did she learn to sing like that in such a short amount of time? She had sounded amazing.

"I thought you said Lila couldn't sing," Mandy said to Jessica with a suspicious look on her face.

"Her dad probably flew in a voice teacher from the Metropolitan Opera in New York," Jessica answered weakly.

Mandy shook her head. "You know, Jessica, sometimes this competition thing between you and

Lila gets way out of hand. I know you're jealous of her, but face it, she's got a ton of talent. No matter how many bad things you say about her, it doesn't change the fact that she's got a great voice."

Jessica's mouth dropped. "Mandy!"

"I don't want to hear any more about Lila," Mandy said. "*I'm* going to go congratulate her."

Mandy hurried over to join the crowd that was gathered around Lila. After a few seconds, Jessica heard Lila's voice rising over the excited babble in the auditorium.

"May I have your attention?" Lila shouted. "Everybody is invited to my house tonight for a screening of the video and a party."

Everybody started cheering.

Jessica stood rooted to the stage, her mind working fast and furious. There was something strange about this whole thing. Something very strange.

"We did it!" Lila hissed in almost hysterical happiness, hurrying backstage where Johanna was quietly unhooking her microphone.

Johanna grinned, and the two girls hugged. "It worked," Johanna said thankfully. "I can't believe it worked. I got to sing my own song, but I didn't have to do it in front of an audience."

Johanna's heart was still racing. She'd never sung for a live audience before. It had been incredibly thrilling. And the excitement had brought out textures and colors in her voice that she'd never even known were there.

Judging by the explosion of applause that had erupted as soon as she had finished singing, the results had been stupendous.

Lila held up her hand and Johanna high-fived it. "We make a great team," Lila said. "With your talent and my attitude, we're bound to win the RockTV contest."

Johanna smiled. "I can't wait to see us on the screen tonight."

Lila's face seemed to fall a fraction. "You're coming to the party?"

"Well, sure," Johanna said. "Why wouldn't I?"

"Oh, I just thought that since you were so shy and everything that you wouldn't want to come."

Johanna smiled. "Are you kidding? I wouldn't miss your party for anything. We're a team—right?"

Lila gave her a tight smile. "Right."

"Lila!" someone shouted from the stage area. "Come out here and take another bow."

Eight

◇

"Great party, Lila," Randy said, stuffing another chip into his mouth.

"Lila always gives great parties," Mandy said, reaching for a handful of caramel corn.

Johanna stood a little apart from the group, nervously watching the scene. A few people had complimented her on her song, but most of the attention was focused on Lila, and it looked as if Lila was loving it.

The more attention Lila got, the more confident she became. A little too confident, maybe. Lila was actually beginning to seem a little *arrogant*.

She'd hardly said a word to Johanna all evening, and she hadn't made any effort to include her in any conversations.

"Great job, Lila," Bruce said, brushing past

Johanna without even glancing at her. "You have a gorgeous voice."

"I think you may be the most talented person at Sweet Valley Middle School," Scott added with an admiring smile. "Oh, sorry," he muttered vaguely as he stepped on Johanna's toe.

Randy came rushing into the dining room. "OK, everybody! It's all set up in the den," he said breathlessly. "We're ready to run the video."

Johanna felt her stomach lurch. What if it didn't look convincing on camera? What if people found out what they had done?

Suddenly she was overcome by the feeling that she and Lila had done something wrong and deceitful. She wasn't even sure she wanted to see the video.

She threw another look at Lila, who was surrounded by friends. All of them were complimenting her, and Lila's eyes were shining. She didn't look at all scared or nervous. She looked confident and like she was having fun. She looked full of "attitude."

Johanna swallowed the dry lump in her throat. If she could just talk to Lila, maybe she would feel better. Lila had a way of making this whole thing seem OK.

Nervously she began to thread her way through the crowd. "Excuse me," she whispered. "Excuse me."

"Come on, everybody," Randy called out. "We're screening the video in five minutes."

All the other Unicorns seemed to surround Lila and sweep her out of the dining room, toward the den and the big-screen TV where they were going to watch the video. Johanna managed to reach through the crowd and tap Lila on the shoulder. "Lila," she said.

Lila turned and lifted one eyebrow slightly. "Yes?"

"I need to talk to you," Johanna said.

"Now?" Lila exclaimed. "Can't you see my friends are waiting for me?"

Johanna felt her jaw drop. She wasn't sure she had heard Lila right. "Aren't I your friend?" she asked in low voice.

Lila immediately cut her eyes in the direction of the other girls.

Johanna looked at the circle of snobby faces around Lila. Tamara was staring at her as if she had two heads. Kimberly smothered a giggle behind her hand. She saw Ellen's elbow slightly nudge Janet's rib cage and the two girls exchange a knowing glance.

Johanna felt as though she'd been punched in the stomach. Attitude was one thing. Nerve was another. Anger, resentment, and humiliation all welled up in Johanna's throat, making it feel so tight, she could hardly speak. How could Lila treat her like this? It was as though she actually believed *she* had done the singing. As though she had totally forgotten that Johanna had saved her from being humiliated in front of the entire school.

For a brief moment, Johanna almost considered shouting out the truth. But that would mean she would have to prove it. She would actually have to open her mouth and sing in front of all these hostile and unfriendly people. People who obviously didn't like her. People who obviously thought she was a dork.

"Did you have something to say?" Janet asked impatiently.

"I . . . I . . ." Johanna's mouth was working hard to make some words come out, but it was just impossible with all those people staring at her.

Lila glanced at her watch and tapped her foot. "If you have something to say, Johanna, please say it, so we can get on with the screening."

A snort of derisive laughter escaped Ellen.

Johanna gasped and began to back away. These girls were awful. And Lila was the most awful of them all. She'd used Johanna, tricked her into making her a star, acted as though she wanted to be her friend. And now . . .

"Hey!" Bruce protested as she turned away from the group and practically knocked him over as she ran for the door.

She could hear the laughter and excited chatter of all the other kids as she flung open the front door and lurched out into the night with tears streaming down her face. She wished she'd never heard of Lila Fowler. She wished she'd never heard of the Unicorns. She wished she'd never agreed to write the song.

And most of all, she wished she weren't a dork.

"Fantastic!" Tamara squealed.

"Unbelievable!" Mandy shouted.

All the kids that sat around Lila in the dark room kept telling her how great she was. But Lila couldn't seem to enjoy it. There was a slightly sick, queasy feeling in her stomach. It didn't feel like indigestion. So what was it that was making her feel so bad?

You feel bad because you feel guilty, a little voice in the back of her head answered.

Lila pursed her lips impatiently. It was stupid to feel guilty over somebody like Johanna. She might have a lot of talent and everything, but she was still a dork. Lila was a Unicorn. Surely Johanna hadn't expected that they would still be friends when the video project was over.

Why not? the little voice asked.

"Because I'm a Unicorn and she's a dork," Lila repeated in an insistent tone.

"Did you say something?" Mandy asked over the music.

Lila's cheeks turned pink. Good thing it was too

dark for anyone to see. She hadn't meant to say it out loud. "Uh-uh," she said quickly.

Up on the screen, Randy's camera had zoomed in for a close-up, and Lila watched herself deliver the thrilling last line of Johanna's song. "*I love you sooooo*," came the voice over the speakers, as clear as a bell.

"Wow, Lila," Mandy shouted over the applause. "You are awesome. Our video is definitely going to win the contest."

Lila swallowed hard and nodded.

Jessica stood in the back, eyeing the screen. Was it her imagination, or was there something strange about the video? Something slightly off? And why had Johanna gone rushing out of the party looking so upset?

"Hey, Randy," she said, as he hurried past her. "Do you think I could get a copy of that video for myself?"

Randy frowned. "Geez, Jessica. If I have to start running off copies for everybody, it's going to take me days."

"I'm not just anybody," Jessica protested. "Don't forget, I *did* write the lyrics."

He pushed his glasses up on his nose. "That's true. OK. I'll make a copy for you—but you have to pay for the cassette."

Jessica smiled. "Of course I'll pay for the cassette." *If what I suspect turns out to be true*, she thought, *it'll be money well spent.*

"Here it comes!" Tamara gasped.

"Shhh," Grace ordered.

It was Saturday, the big day. The Unicorns were gathered in the Fowlers' den, glued to the set.

"And now . . ." announced veejay Robert Rowdy, "the moment you've all been waiting for." The camera swooped around to get a good shot of Robert Rowdy's incredibly punked-out hairstyle. Then it zoomed in for a close-up of his face. "The winner of the School Days video competition!" he shouted.

Immediately the screen was filled with a gigantic close-up of Lila.

"Omigod!" Janet screamed.

"All right!" Mandy shouted.

All the Unicorns were screaming and high-fiving one another.

The video was playing now, but Lila could hardly hear it over the shouting.

"There I am!" Tamara screeched.

"And there's Jessica and Grace!" Betsy yelled.

The video played on and on, and Lila could hardly speak, she was so thrilled. It was amazing, but she looked even better on-screen than she remembered. The beads on her short pink dress sparkled as they caught the light. Her long hair spun around her face in a slow-motion halo. Her dance moves were perfectly timed. She looked even *better* than Melody Power.

Suddenly all the little feelings of guilt she had felt about Johanna disappeared. If Johanna had sung the song herself, they couldn't have won. Johanna was shy and awkward and not nearly as pretty as Lila. No way could they have won the audio-video system with Johanna out in front.

Abruptly the video ended, and all the girls applauded. Robert Rowdy appeared again on-screen. "That was Lila Fowler at Sweet Valley Middle School," he said. He shook his head in amazement. "You know, that video is great. The camera work is good. The musicians and backup singers and dancers are all terrific. But let's face it: That girl has about the most gorgeous voice in California."

Lila's heart was beginning to beat with a slow, sickening thud.

Robert Rowdy smiled into the camera. "I've never heard a voice that professional on a performer as young as Lila Fowler. That's why I'm entering her video into our New Voices contest. In case you're not familiar with our New Voices competition, that's where viewers from all over California call in to let us know which new performer they liked best that they've seen on our show."

The Unicorns all began screaming again.

"The winner of the New Voices contest gets to appear on this show—live—next Saturday. So be sure and tune in next Friday afternoon, when the winner is announced on our Friday-afternoon *Rock and Roll for Lunch* show."

Lila's hands flew to her throat in horror.

"You're going to be famous, Lila!" Grace shouted gleefully.

"I'm really proud to be your friend," Tamara said with a smile.

"This is so totally awesome, I can't even think of anything to say," Janet cried.

Lila's face felt hot and flushed. This was awful. This was a nightmare. This was the worst thing she could possibly imagine happening in the whole world.

What if she actually won? What if she actually had to go on RockTV and sing? Suddenly Lila knew exactly how Johanna felt about performing. She felt nervous, sick, and scared out of her wits.

"I love you sooooooo," Lila sang, her face filling the screen of the Wakefields' TV.

Jessica caught her breath with an excited gasp and pressed the remote to turn off the VCR.

It was Sunday, and she'd watched "Unicorn Rock" a hundred times now. She'd finally noticed something very strange. When she watched in slow motion, she could see that Lila's voice didn't *exactly* match up with the movements of her mouth.

Oh, it was close. Very close. But the voice and the mouth definitely did not match. Jessica didn't know how she'd managed to pull it off, but Lila Fowler wasn't singing on that tape. And that would explain why she had looked less than thrilled when she'd heard she was being entered in the New Voices contest. It would also explain why she'd developed such a beautiful voice in such an incredibly short time.

"Wait till Elizabeth sees this," Jessica said excitedly, thundering up the stairs.

"Would you please get off my bed," Elizabeth begged in a thick, wheezing voice.

Jessica pulled at the sleeve of Elizabeth's nightgown. "But I need you to come downstairs and look at something on the VCR. I've been suspicious about something for a while now. I think I finally have all the proof I need."

Elizabeth groaned and turned over. "Would you please leave me alone?" she asked miserably. "You're as bad as Amy."

"What do you mean, I'm as bad as Amy?"

"Ever since she read that book by Carl Birnbaum, she's been driving me crazy with her investigative reporting. First she wanted to write an exposé on unsanitary conditions in the school cafeteria. She said the garbage cans were dirty. I told her of course they're dirty. They're full of garbage.

That's why they call them garbage cans."

Jessica giggled. "That is pretty stupid."

Elizabeth blew her nose into a tissue. "Then she called and said she had a great idea for an exposé on Mr. Clark."

Jessica's eyes widened. "Oh, no. What?"

"She saw somebody on *America's Meanest Escaped Convicts* who looked like Mr. Clark—if he were wearing a beard, a wig, and sunglasses."

"Doesn't everybody in a beard, wig, and sunglasses look pretty much alike?" Jessica asked.

"Yes!" Elizabeth sat back in her bed with a sigh. "I really don't think Mr. Clark is an escaped convict."

"Noooo," Jessica agreed. "But he can be pretty mean sometimes."

Elizabeth shook her head. "Amy's just determined to write an exposé. The *Sixers* is supposed to come out tomorrow, and she's worried that she doesn't have an exciting story for the front page. I told her the 'Unicorn Rock' story was a great front-page piece. But she says it's just publicity fluff for the Unicorns. She wants a juicy scandal to write about."

"Well, I just may have one for her," Jessica said excitedly. "And if you'll just come downstairs with me and look at something on the VCR, you'll . . ."

Elizabeth didn't let her finish. She groaned and pulled the covers up higher. "Please don't tell me any more about it. I don't feel well. I don't want to watch TV. And I don't want to hear about anymore scandals."

"But . . ."

"Go away!" Elizabeth begged, pulling the covers up over her head.

"Jessica, leave your sister alone," Mrs. Wakefield ordered as she came into the room with a tray of orange juice, aspirin, and cough medicine. "In fact, I think you should stay out of her room until she's well. I don't want you catching the flu. And if Amy calls, tell her Elizabeth can't talk."

"Tell her to write whatever she wants," Elizabeth said in a muffled voice from beneath the covers. "She's in charge."

"OK," Jessica muttered. Elizabeth was so cranky when she was sick. Maybe it was better just to leave her alone. Besides, she wasn't in any position to help Jessica; she couldn't get the paper out if she was sick in bed.

Suddenly Jessica's face broke into a broad smile. *Elizabeth* couldn't get the paper out, but Amy could. Hadn't Elizabeth just said that *Amy was in charge*?

"Don't worry about a thing," she said soothingly to Elizabeth. "You just get some rest and don't worry about the *Sixers*."

Before Elizabeth could answer, Jessica was out the door and in the hall, dialing Amy Sutton's number.

Nine

"Daddy," Lila said that night at dinner. "It's been a long time since we've been to Paris. Why don't we go?"

Mr. Fowler sat across from her at the dinner table, a distracted frown on his face. "What was that, honey?"

"I said, why don't we go to Paris?" Lila repeated.

"I've been to Paris several times in the last year," her father answered. "I don't think I'd enjoy going again anytime soon."

"How about London, then? Or Rome? And I hear Switzerland is really beautiful."

Mr. Fowler smiled. "I didn't realize you were so interested in European travel, Lila."

"Oh," Lila breathed, "I am. Really. I'm just dying to go to Europe."

"Well, then, we'll go."

"Oh, thank you, Daddy. Thank you. Thank you," she said, almost crying with relief.

"Europe is beautiful in the summer," her father said.

"Summer!" Lila cried. "I don't want to go next summer."

Mr. Fowler frowned. "When did you want to go?"

"Next weekend."

Mr. Fowler laughed. "I'm afraid that's impossible."

"But I have to go next weekend," Lila wailed. "I've got to get away—far away."

Her father shook his head. "Lila, I'm afraid a trip to Europe next weekend is simply out of the question. It's logistically impossible. You have school. And even if you didn't, I couldn't, for business reasons."

"What business reasons?" Lila demanded.

"I was forced to dismiss an employee today for plagiarism, and I've got to find someone to replace him. In fact, on Tuesday I'll be flying to New York for several days to conduct interviews with possible replacements."

"What's plagiarism?" Lila asked.

"That's when you try to pass someone else's work off as your own," Mr. Fowler answered with a grim look on his face.

Lila's stomach began to churn. Why did she

have to hear about this *now*? "Is that really such a bad thing to do?" she asked in a small voice.

"I think so," Mr. Fowler said. "When someone works hard on something, and then somebody else tries to take credit for it, that's dishonest. It's like being a thief. And I won't have any thieves in my organization."

"May I be excused?" Lila whispered, pushing her plate away. Suddenly her appetite was gone.

Johanna sighed deeply. It was late Sunday night and she was in her nightgown—the one that had little musical notes embroidered on the sleeves. She was lying in bed, trying to read a magazine. But really, she was just staring into space and feeling miserable. She had tried to fall asleep, but every time she closed her eyes, she saw all the Unicorns sneering at her.

The article she was reading was about Melody Power. There was a picture of Melody singing in front of a huge audience full of adoring fans. Seeing that picture made Johanna feel even worse. All the people at the party on Friday evening had looked at Lila just the way Melody Power's adoring fans looked at her. And Lila had looked at Johanna—the real star—as if she were a bug.

There was a soft knock at the door.

"Come in," Johanna said.

The door opened and Julie stuck her head in.

"You're still awake," she said happily, coming into the room. "I thought you'd be asleep, but I saw the light on under your door."

"I couldn't sleep," Johanna answered. She glanced at the clock on the bedside table. "Wow, your rehearsal ran really late."

"Tell me about it," Julie said, flopping down on the edge of Johanna's bed. "Hey! By the way, congratulations! The first violinist told me the Sweet Valley Middle School video won the RockTV School Days competition. He also said that Robert Rowdy entered Lila Fowler in the New Voices contest."

Johanna nodded and closed her magazine.

Julie shook her head. "Johanna, I really wish you weren't so shy about performing. I haven't seen the video, but I can't believe that Lila has a better voice than you do."

"She doesn't," Johanna said quietly.

"Then doesn't that tell you something?" Julie asked. "Doesn't that tell you that you should be out there performing? You said that Lila can't sing at all. If somebody who can't sing can win a contest, just think how well somebody like you—who *can* sing—would do."

Johanna felt too miserable to answer.

"Don't look so unhappy," Julie said with a sigh. "I won't nag anymore, I promise. Besides, I'm too sleepy." She stood up and yawned, stretching her arms above her head. "See you in the morning."

"Good night," Johanna said as Julie softly shut the door. Johanna closed her eyes and sighed. Maybe Julie was right. Maybe she should be out there performing.

It had been such a thrill to sing her own song live. She'd never felt so good about herself before. She'd loved the experience of singing for an audience—*as long as I was safely hidden from view*, she thought unhappily.

Johanna flopped back against her pillows with a groan.

She hated herself for letting Lila Fowler take advantage of her. She hated herself for trusting Lila and for being such a coward.

If her voice actually won the contest, what would Lila do then? What would Johanna do?

If only Lila hadn't turned out to be such a jerk. This whole situation wouldn't be nearly as awful if they could talk about it; put their heads together and figure out what to do. Be a team.

Johanna pulled the covers up over her face and let out another groan. *I wonder what Lila is thinking right now.*

"No," Lila moaned, tossing in her sleep. "No."

A part of her brain kept trying to tell her to wake up, that she was having a nightmare. But she couldn't wake up, so she had to keep running . . . and running . . .

"Stop, thief!" Mandy Miller shouted.

"Stop that girl! Stop her. She stole Johanna Porter's voice!" someone else bellowed.

Lila was running so fast, her lungs felt as if they were going to explode. She turned and saw Randy Mason, Maria Slater, and several of the Unicorns chasing her.

"Stop, thief!" Mandy shouted again.

Lila ducked into the doorway of a music store and hid behind the door as everyone went racing past.

"Whew!" she breathed in relief as they disappeared.

"May I help you?" a voice asked.

Lila turned and her jaw dropped. "Robert Rowdy?"

"Yes," he said. Then he frowned. "Say, aren't you Lila Fowler?"

"Yes," Lila squeaked. "Do you know me?"

Robert Rowdy's face grew dark and angry. "I sure do. I saw your face on a Wanted poster in the post office. You're wanted in Sweet Valley for stealing Johanna Porter's voice."

Lila gasped. "I really didn't mean to do anything wrong."

"Do you expect us to believe that you didn't mean to trick Johanna into thinking you were her friend?" he demanded.

Suddenly Lila was standing in the witness stand of a courtroom.

Robert Rowdy was the prosecuting attorney. The other Unicorns were in the jury box. *The judge was her very own father.*

"Daddy," she pleaded.

"Don't you *Daddy* me," he warned, shaking his gavel in her direction.

"Do you expect us to believe that you didn't mean to let people think that the beautiful voice they were hearing was yours?" Robert Rowdy thundered.

"Booooo!" the Unicorns in the jury box shouted.

"Do you expect us to believe that you didn't mean to steal all the credit?"

"Boooooo!" all the people in the courtroom shouted.

"Lila Fowler, you're a liar and a thief."

"She's guilty!" the Unicorns yelled from the jury box.

"She's guilty!" Mr. Fowler echoed.

"But, Daddy . . ." Lila cried again.

"Keep quiet," Mr. Fowler said sternly. *WHAP!* He smacked the gavel on his desk. "I, Mr. Fowler, do hereby sentence you, Lila Fowler, to . . ."

Lila leaped out of the witness stand and ran out of the courtroom into a long hallway.

"Stop her!" she heard someone shout from inside the courtroom. Several pairs of feet began to pound down the hallway behind her.

"She's a phony," Randy yelled.

"She's a liar!" Maria shouted.

"She's a no-talent!" Jessica howled gleefully. "She should have let me be the lead singer."

"Catch her!" they all screamed.

Lila turned a corner, ran into a room, and gasped. "Johanna!"

Johanna sat at a piano. She lifted her head and stared coolly at Lila. "Yes?"

"Hide me," Lila begged. "Please hide me."

The sound of the angry crowd was getting closer.

"Why should I?" Johanna asked. "You're not my friend. You just pretended you were." She got up from the piano bench and ran to the door. "Lila's in here!" she shouted into the hall.

"No!" Lila cried. "No!"

The crowd rushed in and grabbed her. Maria tugged on her arms, and Jessica grabbed her legs.

"No!" Lila cried. "Stop!" She struggled as hard as she could, twisting her body out of their grasp, and . . .

Wham!

. . . Lila woke up as soon as she hit the floor.

She blinked her eyes groggily. She'd struggled so hard in her dream that she'd twisted right out from under the covers and off the edge of the bed.

"What a nightmare!" she moaned. "What an awful, horrible, nightmare." And what an awful, horrible fix she was in. All because she was an awful, horrible person.

Slowly Lila climbed back into bed and under the covers. What had made her treat Johanna so badly? she wondered miserably. Why had she let all that undeserved praise go to her head? What had made her think she had a right to claim someone else's talent as her own?

"Because I'm a Unicorn and she's a dork?" Lila asked aloud in the dark.

It sounded pretty lame.

Ten

If one more person congratulates me, I'll start scream-ing, Lila thought unhappily.

It was Thursday, and she'd lost count of the number of people who had told her how wonderful she was and how proud they were to know her. Her cheeks felt stiff from smiling all week when what she really felt like doing was hiding under a rock.

The door to the girls' bathroom opened, and Lila held her breath. She let it out in relief when she saw it was Maria, and not Johanna.

"Good for you, Lila," Maria said happily. "You're getting a break into the business most people would kill for."

"Really?" Lila croaked.

"Sure. Getting entered in the New Voices contest is a big deal."

"Yeah," Lila said, "but I probably won't win."

"Well, even if you don't, it's still an incredible achievement to get this far. You should be really proud of yourself."

Lila didn't feel proud of herself at all.

At the end of the hall, she caught a glimpse of Johanna at her locker. As usual, she was by herself, standing with her shoulders hunched and her hair hanging in her eyes as if she was trying to hide.

Just then Johanna turned, and Lila caught a glimpse of her face. It was hurt, angry, and most of all, sad.

Immediately Lila dropped her eyes. She couldn't even stand to look Johanna in the face.

"Geez, Lila," Betsy said. "You look awful."

"I feel awful," Lila muttered.

"I don't blame you," Betsy said. "It's the suspense. It's killing everybody. Even some of the teachers are biting their nails."

Janet patted Lila on the shoulder. "Try to relax. I know there's a lot of competition, but I can't believe anybody's got a voice as good as yours. You'll definitely win."

Lila's stomach lurched. Today was the day. At twelve thirty Robert Rowdy was going to announce the winner of the New Voices competition.

"Of course she's going to win," Grace said with

a smile. "And we'll all be watching her live on RockTV tomorrow."

Lila's stomach began to do somersaults.

"Tamara talked Ms. Laster into letting her watch the TV in the library during lunch so that we'll know as soon as the winner is announced," Janet said.

"Great," Kimberly said. "Come on, Lila, let's go to the cafeteria. Your public is waiting for you."

"Can't you even eat some Jell-O?" Grace asked.

Lila shook her head and looked at her watch. It was almost noon, and the cafeteria was packed. All around her, people were darting looks at her. Several people gave her the thumbs-up sign.

Please don't let me win the contest, she pleaded silently. *Please don't let me win.*

Her eyes swept the cafeteria. Sitting alone, at a table on the other side of the cafeteria, was Johanna.

I'll bet she hates me, Lila thought. *I bet she feels just as awful as I do. What a mess. If only I hadn't been so mean to her. It wouldn't be so bad if we were in this together.*

Suddenly the door to the cafeteria burst open, and Tamara stood breathlessly in the doorway. "The results are in!" she shouted. *"Lila won the New Voices competition!"*

A cheer went up in the cafeteria.

Just then Amy Sutton came barreling into the

room with a stack of newspapers under her arm and Jessica trailing behind her. "Hold it!" she shouted, pushing past Tamara.

But the shouts and cheering were still deafening.

"Be quiet!" Jessica shouted. "Amy has something to say!"

Amy climbed up on a table, and the cafeteria fell silent. "Before you get too excited, you should know the truth. This whole video project is a fraud," she said angrily. She began to shove newspapers into people's hands. "But I'll let you read about it for yourselves."

"'Lila Fowler Involved in Lip-Syncing Scandal!'" Bruce read out loud. "Amy! Are you out of your mind?"

Lila's head was spinning. This moment was far, far worse than she had dreamed. There was nothing that could happen to her for the rest of her life that would ever be as bad as this.

"This is all lies, Amy," Grace protested. "Tell them, Lila."

"No way could Lila have pulled off something like this. We would have known about it," Scott said.

"Jessica is just jealous of Lila." Kimberly turned and glared at Jessica, who was still handing out papers.

"I can't believe you two would do this," Mandy said angrily.

Janet tapped a spoon on a glass of water. "Could everybody please shut up for a minute!" She waited for most of the noise to die down. "Lila's a Unicorn. A Unicorn would never stoop so low. There's no way she could have faked this. Pay no attention to . . . to . . ." Janet frowned at Jessica. "To rejected wannabe lead singers."

"It's not a lie!" Jessica insisted. "If you don't believe me, *ask Johanna Porter*."

Every single eye in the cafeteria looked toward Johanna.

Lila's eyes widened as Johanna stood slowly and began walking toward the group. Her eyes were fixed on Lila's face. Lila gulped and stood up a little straighter. Her heart was hammering against her rib cage. OK, she was about to be totally exposed as a phony. But in a way, it would be a relief to have it over with. It was like Johanna said—having talent was a big responsibility. Too big. Especially when you were faking it. "Johanna," Amy began, "is that Lila singing on the video?"

There was a long pause.

Johanna's mouth opened, then closed.

"Well?" Amy pressed. "Is it or isn't it?"

Johanna's eyes locked on Lila's again. Lila's heart was beating so fast, she felt as if her chest might explode.

The entire cafeteria was completely silent.

"Of course it's Lila," Johanna said calmly. "I

should know. I'm the one who taught her the song."

"Gee, thanks, Jessica," Amy said sarcastically as she stormed down the hallway.

"I'm right," Jessica insisted, practically running to keep up with her. "I know I'm right. I don't care what Johanna says."

Amy skidded to a stop, turned, and scowled at Jessica. "You made a total fool out of me—*and* yourself. And you ruined the credibility of the *Sixers*. So just stop it, OK?" She leaned against a nearby wall and smacked her hand to her forehead. "Elizabeth is going to kill me when she finds out. My first chance at being editor in chief, and I blow it by printing a totally false and *malicious* accusation."

"But . . ." Jessica began.

"Please don't tell me anything else," Amy begged. "Right now I've got to think about how to explain this to Elizabeth."

Jessica sighed and bit her lip as she watched Amy hurry away. Suddenly she heard Kimberly's and Janet's voices coming up the hallway. She ran around the corner.

No way did she want to face Janet now—Janet was furious at her. The low murmur of their voices got louder as they got nearer. Jessica flattened herself against the wall to keep from being seen as they walked by. But instead of continuing down the hall, they stopped a few feet from where Jessica was standing.

"Oh, Janet," she heard Kimberly gasp. "That's horrible. Does anybody else know?"

"No," Janet said in a hushed voice. "And if anybody ever finds out, it'll ruin my life. Promise you won't tell?"

"I promise," Kimberly agreed.

"Thanks, Kimberly. I had to tell somebody, and I knew I could trust you."

"So, when . . ." Kimberly began.

"Saturday," Janet answered quickly. "I'll be at Lila's in the morning to see her off to Los Angeles. Then I'll slip away a few minutes after she leaves. You try to keep the others from noticing I'm gone or asking me any questions."

Jessica drew in her breath. *Horrible secret! Scandal! Saturday!* She pursed her lips. So! There *was* a scandal. And somehow Janet Howell was mixed up in it.

A Unicorn would never stoop so low. Ha!

"Amy!" Jessica called out. "Wait up!"

Eleven

"I can't believe you did that!" Lila gasped. "Why? I thought you'd hate me."

Johanna shrugged. "I did. But in a weird way, I still think of you as my friend. You were in a tight spot, and I didn't want to let you down."

"But I let you down," Lila said quietly. She looked up at Johanna's serious face. "I'm really sorry about that. I wish there were something I could do to make it up to you. Is there anything I could buy you?" she asked hopefully. "I really owe you one."

Lila and Johanna were sitting alone at one of the lunch tables. Most of the other kids had already left the cafeteria after congratulating Lila. Now the two girls were finally getting a chance to talk.

Johanna smiled. "No. I can't really think of anything I want you to buy me. But it's nice of you to offer."

"Well, I appreciate your covering for me. Now, if we can just figure out a way to get out of RockTV, we'll both be in the clear. I guess I could fake laryngitis or something."

"But I don't want you to get out of RockTV," Johanna said.

Lila's jaw dropped. "What do you mean? *I* can't go on TV and sing live," she argued. "I'll be totally humiliated."

"No," Johanna agreed. "But *we* can."

"How?" Lila cried. "And why?"

Johanna's face flushed. "I loved singing for an audience. It was the most exciting thing I've ever done. And the audience loved me. At least, they loved my voice. But I'm afraid if they saw the person who was really singing, they wouldn't like it as much. Let's face it," she said softly, "I'm not all that pretty. I don't have many friends. And, well . . . I'm kind of a dork."

Lila felt awful. She couldn't even argue with Johanna, because everything she was saying was true. With all her heart, Lila wished she could do something to help Johanna. But the scheme Johanna had in mind was nuts. "Look, Johanna," she began, "I understand how you feel. But we'd never be able to pull the same stunt twice. I mean, how would we even explain your coming to the studio with me?"

Johanna's mouth formed a determined line. "I don't know," she said. "But you'll figure something out."

"*I'll* figure something out?" Lila demanded.

Johanna nodded and grinned. "You said you wished there was something you could do. Well, this is it."

Lila groaned. "I was afraid you were going to say that." She bent down and put her head in her hands. "OK. OK. Just let me think a minute."

"Your hairdresser! Can't you think up something else? How many twelve-year-old singers show up with their own hairdresser?" Johanna asked.

"How many twelve-year-old singers show up with their own Rolls Royce and driver?" Lila countered, pushing Johanna into the door of Cut and Snip, her favorite salon. "And even if they do think it's weird—what's the alternative? I can't exactly introduce you as my *voice*. Now, come on, you're the one who's determined to go through with this. So how about a little cooperation?"

"Well, even if I do say I'm your hairdresser," Johanna argued, "I still don't see why *I* have to get all done up."

"Are you kidding?" Lila said. "If you're going to pose as a celebrity hairdresser, you're going to have to look like one. You're going to have to act like one too. And that means you're going to have to start developing some *attitude*."

The two girls hurried over to the reception desk, where a glamorous-looking lady sat with a large book spread out in front of her.

"Hi, Gladys," Lila said with a smile.

"Hello, Lila," Gladys responded. "Here for a haircut?"

Lila nodded. "Both of us need the works."

Gladys frowned at her appointment book. "I don't see your names down here. Did you have an appointment?"

Johanna immediately began to feel shy and embarrassed. "We can come back later," she said in barely a whisper.

"Appointment?" Lila laughed breezily. "How could I make an appointment when I didn't know I was going to be in the mood for a haircut today?"

Gladys laughed.

"And besides," Lila cajoled her, "since when does a famous video star and a famous songwriter need an appointment?"

Gladys looked at Johanna. "Did you write that beautiful song I saw Lila sing on RockTV?"

Johanna began to blush. "Yes," she whispered, looking down at her shoes.

Lila nudged her with her elbow. "Attitude," she whispered.

Johanna stood up a little straighter. She tried to unhunch her shoulders.

"My, you girls are certainly talented." Gladys winked at Lila. "I'll see what I can do to squeeze you two in."

"Thanks, Gladys," Lila said.

Lila led Johanna over to the waiting area. "See? It's all about attitude."

"Now, that's what I call hair with attitude," Lila said, looking at Johanna in the mirror.

"I can't believe it," Johanna said.

Lila's favorite hairdresser, Roland, had cut Johanna's red hair in long, measured layers. Then he'd blown and curled and crimped it into a long, thick mass of flowing curls.

"I look like a rock star," Johanna whispered.

"Mademoiselle is pleased?" Roland asked.

Johanna swallowed. "I'm not sure it's me."

"It's not yet," Lila said happily. "But it will be."

"You're really going to lend me these clothes?" Johanna said with a gasp.

"Sure." Lila pulled a very expensive-looking outfit from the closet. "Lila Fowler's hairdresser has got to look sharp." She handed the outfit to Johanna.

Johanna held the spangled purple dress up in front of her and stared at herself in the mirror. She smiled. "I look like a completely different person. I look . . . well . . ." She smiled at Lila. "I look sort of like you."

"Now you've got to learn to act sort of like me," Lila said. "We're about to pull off the most daring stunt in the history of RockTV. That means you're going to have to be able to move around the set, snoop into places you don't belong, and think fast on your feet. You can't weenie out the first time somebody gives you a dirty look and asks you what you're doing with that microphone."

Lila flipped her hair over her shoulder and swaggered across her bedroom. "You gotta move around that place with some attitude."

She whirled around and grinned at Johanna. "Now you try it."

Johanna laughed and did her best to imitate the exaggerated confidence of Lila's walk.

"That's it!" Lila shouted. "That's it. Now let's try it to music." Lila ran over and flipped a button on her CD player. Immediately, pounding rock music filled the room.

"Move around like this," Lila commanded, tossing her head back and forth.

Johanna moved her head to the music.

"Now add the arms," Lila shouted.

Johanna began to swing her arms, synchronizing the movement with her steps.

Pretty soon the girls were laughing and strutting around the room to the beat of the music.

"It's like a dance," Johanna giggled.

"It is a dance," Lila said with a smile. "It's called *The Attitude*."

Twelve

"We'll all be watching, Lila," Janet said.

"Don't forget, we were your friends before you got famous," Betsy joked.

"Got the tape of the music?" Grace asked anxiously.

It was Saturday morning, and all the Unicorns had gathered at Lila's house to see her off to Los Angeles. The backseat of the Fowlers' Rolls Royce contained a large suitcase full of makeup, hot rollers, hair spray, and clothing.

Lila swallowed. "Thanks for the send-off, guys," she said, climbing into the Rolls.

"Here." Grace handed her a little purple flower. "This is for luck. We'll all be watching."

"You are the luckiest girl in the whole world," Tamara sighed.

I'm the most nervous girl in the whole world, Lila thought. But as the car pulled out of the drive, she pushed her nervousness out of her mind. Johanna was depending on her. She couldn't lose her nerve now.

"Richard," she said to the chauffeur as they came to the end of her street. "We're going to make a stop before we head into L.A. We've got to pick up my . . . uh . . . hairdresser."

Amy and Jessica peered out from behind the high hedge that lined the sidewalk across from the Fowler mansion.

"There goes Lila," Jessica whispered.

"And there goes Janet," Amy whispered back.

Jessica parted the branches and peered out. Most of the Unicorns were standing in a cluster, talking excitedly. None of them seemed to notice that Janet had quietly backed away from the group and scooted down the street.

"You're sure you heard them right?" Amy asked for about the fifteenth time.

"Amy!" Jessica exclaimed.

"Well, I don't want to make the same mistake twice. We already look like complete idiots. And when Elizabeth gets back to school and finds out, she's going to kill us."

"No, she won't," Jessica argued. "Because by the time she gets back, we'll be onto the real story behind the Lila Fowler video scandal. After what I overheard, I just know that Janet is at the bottom of all this. If we follow her, we'll have the biggest, juiciest exposé in Sweet Valley's history."

Clank! Clank! Clank!

"What's that knocking noise?" Lila asked with a frown.

Richard, the Fowlers' new chauffeur, shook his head in confusion. "I don't know. I had everything checked before we left Sweet Valley. I can't imagine what's making that sound."

"Gosh," Johanna said, looking nervously out the window. "This would be a horrible place to have car trouble."

They were on the freeway, halfway between Sweet Valley and Los Angeles. Cars and trucks were streaming all around them.

Lila looked at her watch. They still had plenty of time to get into the city and locate the studio.

Just then the car began to cough and sputter. Johanna's eyes grew large. "Oh, no," she moaned. "There's definitely something wrong with the car."

Richard drove onto the shoulder of the road and braked to a stop. "Now, don't panic, girls. I'm sure that no matter what's wrong, I can fix it in a jiffy."

"What is she doing now?" Amy asked.

"She's staring at herself in a window and smiling," Jessica whispered. "It's like she's inspecting her teeth."

"Why would she be inspecting her teeth?" Amy hissed.

"Shhhh," Jessica warned. "She's going into that building. Come on."

Both girls waited until the double glass doors of the office building closed behind Janet before they hurried in.

Ding!

They caught a last glimpse of her as the elevator doors closed.

"Come on!" Jessica urged.

She and Amy hurried over to the elevator and watched the numbers above the door counting off the floors. It paused on ten, and then began to count down again as the elevator returned to the lobby.

"She's on the tenth floor," Amy said, going over to the building directory that was posted on the wall. "Let's see . . ." She traced her finger down the businesses listed on the tenth floor. "Dr. Appleby, GP . . . Arnswell Industries . . . Broadcast Satellite Technologies . . . Dr. Bailey, D.D.S . . ."

Amy gasped. "Wait a minute. *Broadcast Satellite Technologies!* So that's it!"

"What's it?" Jessica asked.

"I saw a movie like this—a movie about spies. It all revolved around satellite technology. Satellite technology is amazing. You can transmit messages and signals and all kinds of things all over the world."

"What are you saying?"

"This probably sounds crazy, but I think somehow, Janet is going to sing for Lila. She's going to transmit her voice via satellite to the studio in Los Angeles."

"I know there's something fishy going on," Jessica said. "But that seems pretty farfetched. Janet and Lila couldn't pull off something that complicated. Lila can't even work her curling iron. A satellite! Get real."

"I'm serious," Amy said. "With Lila's money, she could probably buy ten satellites." Suddenly her eyes grew huge. "Look at that!"

She grabbed Jessica's arm and pulled her over to a little bronze plaque that was mounted on the wall of the lobby.

THIS BUILDING OWNED AND OPERATED BY FOWLER PROPERTIES, INC.

Amy clutched Jessica's hand. "This story is big, Jessica. Really big."

"Three hours!" Johanna cried.

"But we don't have three hours," Lila protested as Richard replaced the receiver of the car phone.

Richard wiped his brow with his handkerchief. "I'm sorry, girls. I really am. According to the motor club, all their repair units are out on call. I'm afraid there's nothing to do but wait and hope they get here sooner."

"Well, I guess that's that," Johanna said in a small, sad voice.

"But . . . but . . ." Lila looked right and left. Cars were whizzing by. She looked down the bank of the freeway, and her eyes widened. At the bottom of the incline was a bus stop. Moving slowly along the road below was a bus. "Los Angeles" it said on the front.

"Come on!" Lila yelled, jumping out of the back-seat and grabbing the bag that held her hot rollers, makeup, and extra clothes.

"What are you doing?" Johanna cried.

"We're taking the bus," Lila announced, jumping over the railing on the side of the freeway and beginning to run down the incline. "Come on."

"Miss Fowler!" Richard shouted behind her. "Lila! Where are you going? Come back here! Your father will kill me for letting you go off by yourself!"

"I'm not by myself!" Lila called over her shoulder. "I'm with Johanna. We'll be fine. Meet us at the studio later when the car is fixed. Come on, Johanna!"

At the bottom of the incline, she could see people boarding the bus.

Johanna was running beside her now. "Do you know your way around L.A. by bus?" she asked breathlessly.

"No," Lila said. "But we'll figure it out as we go. The first step is to get into Los Angeles. Once we get there, we can . . . *Yikes!*" she cried as she tripped over some twisted metal debris that was hidden in the tall grass.

She pitched forward and fell. The suitcase sprang open and the contents scattered in every direction. Lila scrambled to her feet and discovered that the hem of her skirt was caught on the metal. "Oh, no!" she muttered, leaning over to try to unhook her skirt.

Ahead of her, she saw Johanna pause. At the bottom of the incline, the last passenger was getting on the bus.

Lila tugged again at her skirt, but it was really stuck.

Johanna began to run back to help her.

"I'll be OK!" Lila shouted. "Just get on the bus and make him wait! It could be hours till the next one comes."

Johanna paused uncertainly.

"Make the bus wait!" Lila shouted again.

Thirteen

Johanna ran toward the bus and threw herself in the doorway. "Wait!" she managed to gasp.

The bus driver scowled at her. "This is a bus, not a taxi. That means I don't wait. I've got a schedule to keep, so either get on the bus or get off of it."

Every person in the bus was scowling at her, and Johanna felt her ears turning red. "Please wait," she whispered. "My friend is coming any second."

"We're late already," the bus driver snapped.

"But we have to get to Los Angeles," Johanna cried tearfully.

"We *all* have to get to Los Angeles," a cranky woman barked.

If only Lila were doing the talking, Johanna thought. Suddenly Johanna held up her head, threw back her shoulders, and came to a quick decision. Lila had borrowed Johanna's voice. Why shouldn't Johanna borrow Lila's attitude?

"For your information," Johanna said, "my friend and I happen to be the hottest new singing team in Los Angeles. As a matter of fact, we're on our way to perform on RockTV."

The people on the bus broke into laughter.

Johanna's heart was beating fast, but she tossed her hair back off of her shoulders just like Lila. "In fact," she went on, "if you don't wait, you'll regret it for the rest of your life, because you could have bragged to all your friends that you drove the bus with Lila Fowler . . . and . . . and . . . *the fabulous Johanna Porter*." With that, Johanna threw out her arms and posed like Melody Power.

The bus driver began to chuckle. "OK. OK. You win, little lady."

There was a burst of applause as Lila came panting up the steps behind Johanna. "I'm here," she said breathlessly.

Johanna dropped a fistful of change into the meter, and she and Lila quickly found two seats in the back.

The man behind Johanna tapped her on the shoulder. "So which one are you?" he asked with a twinkle in his eye. "Lila Fowler or Johanna Porter?"

"Johanna Porter," she answered. "The *fabulous* Johanna Porter."

"I'm starving," Lila said as the girls stepped

off the bus in the middle of Los Angeles.

"Me too," Johanna said. She looked at her watch. "We've got an hour before we're supposed to be at the studio. I don't think I can sing on an empty stomach."

"And I don't think I can lip-sync on an empty stomach," Lila said with a smile.

They stood at a busy intersection, full of hotels, shops, and restaurants. Pedestrians hurried in every direction.

"Let's go to the dining room of the Ridgemont Hotel," Lila suggested. "We passed it a couple of blocks back."

"That sounds pretty expensive," Johanna said. "And actually, I used all my money on the bus."

"No problem," Lila said, reaching into her purse for her wallet. "I've always got plenty of . . . *oh, no!*" she wailed.

"What's the matter?"

"My wallet. It's gone. I'll bet it's still in the car." Lila sank down on a bench. "That means we not only don't have money for lunch, we don't have money for a cab to the studio, either."

Johanna groaned. She looked around at the people who were rushing by, hoping to see a familiar face. Next to a fountain across the street sat a boy with long hair, playing the guitar. His guitar case lay open on the ground beside him. In the bottom of the case were coins and a few bills.

As the girls watched, the boy strummed his guitar, and a passerby dropped a quarter into the guitar case.

Lila and Johanna looked at each other. "Are you thinking what I'm thinking?" Lila asked.

Johanna turned pale. "Oh, no."

"Oh, yes," Lila said, grabbing her sleeve. "Do you want to sing on RockTV or don't you?"

Johanna bit her lip.

"Look," Lila said. "I'd do it if I could. But I don't have the talent."

Johanna nodded. Lila would do it. She really would.

". . . *the answer is blowing in the wind*," Johanna sang. She let her voice waver a bit, then trail softly away.

The crowd around the fountain burst into enthusiastic applause.

Plink! Plink! Plink!

Quarters and dollar bills began to pile up in the open guitar case. "Wow!" the boy with the long hair cried happily as the crowd began to disburse. "I've never made that kind of money on my own."

Johanna and Lila exchanged a smile. Johanna had just sung three ballads in row, and the crowd had gone crazy. They had applauded and hooted and even demanded an encore.

"My name is Phil," the boy said.

"I'm Lila," Lila said, giving him a flirtatious grin. Phil was definitely cute.

Phil nodded briefly in Lila's direction, but it was clear he had eyes only for Johanna. For once Lila wasn't jealous that somebody else was getting the attention. As a matter of fact, it made her feel great.

"What's your name?" he asked Johanna.

"Johanna Porter," she said with a shy smile.

Phil smiled back, then counted the money and handed her half. "I'm going to remember that. You've got a lot of talent, Johanna Porter."

And pretty soon, Lila thought, *the whole world is going to know it.*

"Here we are," the cab driver said. "RockTV Studios."

"Thanks," Lila said. She handed him enough money to cover the cab ride, and she and Johanna climbed out.

"That was the best lunch I ever had," Johanna said. "And I can't believe the waiter actually gave us a free desert just because we're going to be on RockTV."

"I can't believe you had the nerve to *ask* him for a free desert because we're going on RockTV," Lila said, giggling.

"It was simple." Johanna smiled. "I just pretended I was you. I've been pretending to be you all day."

"I think you might be better at being me than me," Lila said.

Johanna tossed her head, letting her curly hair fly in all directions. "It's called *attitude*," she said with a laugh. She stared up at the tall RockTV building. Abruptly her laughter stopped, and her face turned a little pale.

Lila looked at the imposing entrance, and her face grew serious too.

Johanna's eyelashes fluttered nervously as she turned back to Lila. "No matter what happens now, I just want you to know that I've had more fun today than I've ever had in my whole life."

Lila smiled. "It has been an adventure, hasn't it?"

"I would never have had the nerve to do the things we did if it weren't for you," Johanna said.

Lila took a deep breath and grabbed Johanna's arm, and the two girls walked into the building. A few feet away from the front doors, there was a large security desk. Behind it sat an armed guard. "I'll need you both to sign in," he said.

Johanna picked up the pencil and wrote down both their names, the studio they were going to, and that they were here for the New Voices show.

"Hold it," the security guard barked. He looked down at the ledger. Then he checked a second piece of paper that he kept behind the desk. "Who's this Johanna Porter? I don't see any Johanna Porter on the list. I have just one name down for the New

Voices segment, and that's *Lila Fowler, female, twelve years old.*"

"But we're together," Lila protested. "Johanna Porter is Lila Fowler's personal hairdresser."

The security guard rolled his eyes and laughed. "I never saw a twelve-year-old with a personal hairdresser."

Lila stamped her foot. "I'll bet you never saw a twelve-year-old with a Rolls Royce and driver, either."

"You'd be right," the guard said with a grin. "And I don't see one now. I guess it must be in the shop today, eh?"

"It *is*!" Lila and Johanna shouted together.

The guard laughed. "Listen, girls, I'm sorry. But I have very strict instructions. If your name isn't on the list, you don't go up. All the kids who come on this show want to bring their buddies. But it's a TV show, not a soda shop."

"But . . ." Lila began.

"No buts," the security guard said. "And please don't bother trying to talk your way in, because believe me, it won't work. I've got *one* name on my list. That means *one* of you can go up. Personally, I don't care which one. But whoever goes up there better be ready to sing."

And with that, he sat down behind his desk and opened the newspaper.

*   *   *

"No!" Johanna yelled.

"But you have to, Johanna. You just *have* to," Lila shouted. She was so frustrated, she felt like crying. From the very beginning, she had planned to push Johanna out on the stage when the time came. But she couldn't push her onstage if they couldn't go up to the studio together.

"I won't do it. I absolutely, positively, totally refuse," Johanna shouted over her shoulder as she stomped down the street, ignoring the curious looks of the passersby.

Lila ran to keep up with her. She reached out and grabbed the back of Johanna's blouse, pulling her to a stop. "Please do it, Johanna," she pleaded. "We'll look like total fools if you don't."

Johanna turned. "They're expecting Lila Fowler, remember? You're the one who'll look like a fool if you don't go up there. Not me."

Lila's mouth fell open. "But I can't. I can't go up there alone."

"Well, neither can I," Johanna countered.

"Yes, you can," Lila insisted. "You have the talent. You have the looks." She gave Johanna a pleading smile. "And you'll have me rooting for you all the way." She reached out and took Johanna's hand. "We're a team, remember? I'll just be the invisible partner instead of the silent partner."

Johanna pulled her hand away and clutched her stomach. "I can't do it," she groaned. "Just thinking about it makes me feel like I'm going to throw up."

Lila narrowed her eyes and stared at Johanna. The stare became a glare as Lila's frustration turned to anger. "I've had it with you, Johanna Porter! I thought after the way you were acting today that you had changed. I thought you'd grown up. I thought you'd developed a little attitude. But you haven't changed one bit." She twisted her face into the meanest expression she could manage. "Johanna Porter—you're nothing but a great big *dork*!"

Johanna's pale face began to flush angrily. "I am not," she countered. She took a step toward Lila. "And I have too changed. I'm not going to let you treat me like that anymore . . . you . . . you *jerk*."

Lila lifted her lip in a sneer. "Big talk, *dork*!"

"Quit saying that," Johanna ordered. "I am *not* a dork."

"Oh, yeah?" Lila challenged. "Then *prove* it."

Fourteen

"That's it," Amy gasped. "I can't believe it. It looks almost exactly like the gizmo in the movie. The thingamajig that the master spy used to transmit secret messages."

Jessica could hardly believe her eyes either. Up until now, it hadn't seemed quite real. Amy's theory had seemed farfetched and pretty bizarre.

But now it didn't seem farfetched at all. Janet looked as though she had stepped right out of a science-fiction movie.

Jessica and Amy were hiding behind a large potted plant in the lobby. They had been waiting there for what seemed like hours. Jessica had almost given up hope that Janet was ever going to reappear.

Finally she was coming out of the building. She

was wearing the strangest-looking apparatus on her head that Jessica had ever seen. A leather strap circled the back of her skull and connected pieces of wire that led into her mouth.

Janet looked like a Martian!

"The transmitter is probably in her teeth," Amy whispered as they watched Janet cross the lobby of the building, pause in the doorway for a moment, and then look both ways, as if she were very nervous about being seen.

Then, when the coast seemed clear, she hurried outside.

"Come on," Amy said. "Let's go get our story."

"Janet!" Amy shouted.

"Wait up!" Jessica yelled.

Janet glanced over her shoulder and did a double take when she saw Jessica and Amy. Then she broke into a run.

Amy and Jessica ran after her. "Hold it!" Amy shouted. "We want to talk to you."

After running for several more yards, Janet seemed to change her mind. She skidded to a stop, put her hands on her hips, and spun around to face them.

"All right! All right!" she said angrily. "Now you know. But if you print one word in the paper about this, I'll kill you both."

Amy put her hands on her hips too, and snarled

like a hard-boiled reporter. "Not print it? Are you crazy? Of course I'm going to print it. It's the story of the century. I'll bet you and Lila have broken about a zillion laws with this little scheme of yours. Who do you think you are, anyway?"

"Yeah!" Jessica said, thrusting out her chin like Amy. "Who do you think you are?"

"I'll bet you've even broken some kind of Federal Aviation and Space Program laws," Amy added.

"Yeah!" Jessica said.

Janet's mouth fell open in shock.

"How do you like that, Ms. Lila Fowler?" Amy shouted into Janet's mouth. "We're onto your phony singing scheme."

Janet drew back and stared at Amy as if she had lost her mind. "What are you doing?" she asked, her eyes narrowed and her mouth tight. "And what, may I ask, *are you talking about*?" she finished with a shout.

Amy whipped out her reporter's notebook and pen. "I'm talking about that satellite transmitter you're wearing. We know you were just at Broadcast Satellite Technologies. We know you're the talent and the technology behind the lip-syncing fraud. We know that the Fowlers own that building. In fact, we know everything." Amy squinted her eyes and lifted her lip in a snarl. "There's just one thing I don't understand, Janet. Why are you letting Lila take the credit for your beautiful singing voice? She must be paying you plenty, huh?"

Janet looked at Amy. Then she looked at Jessica. Then she shook her head and took a deep breath. "Read my lips, you *idiots*. This isn't a satellite transmitter. It's my night gear! I just got it at the *orthodontist!*"

"Night gear?" Amy said in stunned surprise.

"Night gear?" Jessica echoed.

"Night gear!" Janet repeated. "As in *to wear at night*. Look. It's for my braces." She opened her mouth wide. "See those little bands and hooks around my back teeth? I'm supposed to wear this thing around my head at night to keep my back teeth from getting crooked."

"If it's night gear, why are you wearing it now— in the middle of the day?" Amy asked, firing the question in a clipped voice. She looked at Jessica and nodded her head as if to say *"Ah ha! Gotcha!"*

"Because it's new and they want me to wear it for a few hours to make sure it's comfortable," Janet shot back. "If it's not, I can go back late this afternoon and have it readjusted."

"Well . . . why were you running away?" Amy demanded suspiciously.

"Would *you* want to be seen wearing something like this?"

Amy and Jessica looked at each other.

Janet had a point, Jessica reflected. Jessica felt herself beginning to blush with embarrassment. Of course it was night gear. She'd seen her cousin in San Diego wearing something similar. Sheesh. She and Amy had really let their imaginations run away with them.

She shot a look at Amy, but Amy still didn't look ready to back down. Her notepad was clutched in her hand and her chin was still stuck defiantly in Janet's face. "How do you explain the fact that Mr. Fowler owns the building?" she demanded, a slight note of desperation creeping into her voice. "That must mean there's a conspiracy with Lila somewhere."

"Mr. Fowler owns half of Sweet Valley," Janet retorted. "He owns tons of office buildings downtown."

Amy groaned. She threw her notebook on the ground and stomped on it. "*Jessica!* You did it again. You got me all fired up about a big scandal and it turned out to be nothing!"

Jessica swallowed hard. She pushed her embarrassment to the side, put her hands on her hips, and lifted her chin stubbornly. Satellite transmitter or no satellite transmitter, something about Lila Fowler's video was fishy. "I don't care," she said through gritted teeth. "Maybe you're not in on Lila's scheme. But I know that Lila Fowler *did not sing that song on the video.*"

"Jessica, give it up, would you?" Janet shouted angrily. "Everybody knows you're just jealous of Lila."

"No, I'm not," Jessica said.

"OK," Amy said agreeably. "You're completely crazy, then."

"No, I'm not!" Jessica yelled.

"Well, then, Ms. Know-it-All-Not-Jealous-and-Not-Crazy," Janet asked nastily, "if Lila didn't sing the song, and *I* didn't sing the song, and *you* didn't sing the song, and *Amy* didn't sing the song, *who did*?"

A man with headphones lifted his hands and spread his fingers wide. Then he began to lower one finger at a time, counting down the seconds.

Johanna stood in the dark area of the sound stage and watched as Robert Rowdy found his mark and positioned himself in front of the first camera.

Suddenly the surge of anger that had propelled Johanna into the office building, up the elevator, and into the studio just minutes before she was due on the air began to fade.

She looked around the studio and saw the technicians scurrying behind the cameras. She saw the director of the show whisper some last-minute instructions to an assistant.

Now that she had stopped feeling angry, she was starting to feel frightened.

"Four . . . three . . . two . . ."

Johanna felt her face begin to flush hotly while her hands turned icy cold. She looked around frantically for an exit sign.

"One . . ." mouthed the technician.

The director nodded at Robert Rowdy, and he broke into a huge smile. "Thanks for joining us," he said in his announcer's voice.

Robert Rowdy's announcer voice was a little different from his speaking voice—not that Johanna had had very long to speak with him. By the time she had arrived upstairs, there had been only a few minutes before show time. Just enough time to shake hands and receive some sketchy instructions about where to stand. Then it was time to shoot.

The next thing she knew, she was standing in the dark, waiting for the cue that Robert Rowdy would give her any second.

Robert Rowdy was still smiling and talking into the camera, explaining how she had won the video contest and gone on to be entered in the New Voices competition.

She tried to follow what he was saying, but it was impossible. All she could hear was something inside her head that sounded like a fire alarm. Her breath seemed to be stuck in her chest, and a cold sweat was breaking out across her brow. She didn't see an exit sign anywhere.

She was trapped!

"I am not a dork!" she heard herself shout as her conversation with Lila replayed itself in her mind.

Why didn't I just admit that I was a dork and go home? Johanna wondered miserably. Why had she let Lila manipulate her again? Manipulate her into doing something she didn't want to do.

Lila was right. She hadn't changed. She hadn't developed any attitude. She was still plain, dorky Johanna Porter, who was too scared and shy to sing her own song in front of an audience. In a matter of seconds, she was going to make a complete and utter fool of herself. Fear was making her mind go blank. She couldn't even remember the first line of the song.

She heard the opening bars of her music being played by the studio musicians.

"And now," Robert Rowdy shouted, "the voice you've all been waiting for!"

Oh no, oh no, oh no. This was it. Total embarrassment. Complete humiliation. *What I am doing?*

As the band came to the last bars of her intro, she quickly closed her eyes. Lila appeared in her mind. The way she stood. The way she projected confidence. The way she tossed her hair when she sang.

She'd pretended to be Lila this afternoon. She'd just have to borrow Lila's personality a little longer.

Johanna took a deep breath, threw back her shoulders, and flipped her hair over her shoulder.

Here goes nothing. She opened her eyes and saw Robert Rowdy's finger pointing in her direction. "You're on," he mouthed.

Johanna drew another deep breath and opened her mouth.

Jessica and Amy sat in the Wakefields' living room with their faces just inches from the TV screen.

The camera swung around, then began to close in on a figure standing in the shadows. The chords built. The drums rolled. As Jessica and Amy scooted up even closer to the screen, the lights came up on . . .

"*JOHANNA PORTER!*" they both screamed.

"*Mom!*" Julie screamed. "Mom! Come down here! Quick!"

Mrs. Porter came running down the stairs. As soon as she reached the bottom step, Julie grabbed her hand and yanked her into the living room. "*Look!*" she shrieked, pointing to the TV.

Mrs. Porter's eyes grew wide. Her hands flew to her mouth in thrilled surprise. "It's Johanna!" she gasped.

Julie pumped her fist in the air as the sound of her sister's beautiful voice filled the living room. "*All right, Johanna!*" she shouted at the top of her lungs.

* * *

"I don't understand!" Tamara gasped as Johanna launched into the last verse of the song. "Where's Lila?"

"Shhhh!" Grace said.

"Quiet!" Mary commanded.

"Unbelievable," Betsy muttered. "Look at her! She's amazing."

The Unicorns were all gathered in Mandy's living room, staring wide-eyed at the TV.

"I can't believe it was Johanna all along!"

"Jessica was right!"

"She looks so beautiful!"

"What an incredible voice!"

Kimberly shook her head regretfully. "I can't believe we ever called her a dork."

"I love you soooooo," Johanna sang, holding the last high, clear note as long as she possibly could.

As soon as the music stopped, the studio crew burst into enthusiastic applause.

Immediately Robert Rowdy came running over and put his arm around her shoulder. "Beautiful work! Incredible! Just incredible. Congratulations!" He shook her hand. "Unfortunately, we're running out of time. So before we go off the air, tell us, Lila, is there anything you'd like us to know about you?"

The studio camera moved in closer, and Johanna

tossed her hair off of her shoulders and smiled into it. "Yes. I'd like you to know that I'm not Lila Fowler. My name is Johanna Porter."

Robert Rowdy looked surprised. "Gee. I thought you looked a little different than you did in your video. But the voice is sure the same. Sounds like there's a story there."

"There is a story," Johanna agreed in a soft, shy voice. "About friendship, actually. And about learning to take big risks. This was really hard for me to do today. I'm pretty shy about performing."

"I never would have guessed," Robert Rowdy said. "You were fabulous."

Johanna smiled. "Thanks. But the credit for that really goes to someone else—one of the most special people I've ever known." She looked into the camera. "Thank you, Lila. A lot of the applause belongs to you."

Fifteen

◇

Lila threw back her head and laughed. "I can't believe Richard got there just in time for me to watch you on the car TV. It was so perfect!"

"It was perfect," Johanna agreed as the two girls approached Sweet Valley in the Fowlers' Rolls Royce.

"You should have seen the guard's face when the Rolls pulled up," Lila said. "I thought he was going to fall over."

"You were really great," Richard called to Johanna from the driver's seat. "I was pretty upset with you girls for running off like that. I was sure you'd get into some kind of trouble." He grinned at Lila and Johanna in the rearview mirror. "I should have known I didn't need to worry about Lila. She's pretty good at looking after herself." He chuckled. "Count on Lila to get exactly what she wants."

"Tell me about it," Johanna said, shaking her head. "She got me to do something I never thought I'd do in a million years." She turned to Lila. "I never would have done it if you hadn't called me a dork."

A rueful smile flickered across Lila's face. "I'm sorry I said that. I don't really think you're a dork." She laughed. "Not anymore, that is."

Johanna laughed too. "Even *I* don't think I'm a dork anymore."

"Listen, if I get to school on Monday and find out I don't have any friends anymore, I can still count on you," Lila said uncertainly. "Right?"

"You bet," Johanna said, reaching over and squeezing her hand. "We're a team. Remember?"

Lila didn't answer. As the car pulled up to the Fowlers' driveway, she was looking out the window, her eyes suddenly round with shock. "I don't think I need to worry about not having any friends," Lila said. "In fact, I don't think either of us needs to worry. Look!"

Johanna couldn't believe it. It looked as though every single kid at Sweet Valley Middle School had gathered in the Fowlers' front yard to welcome them home.

As soon as the crowd saw the car, they started cheering.

Johanna gasped and gripped Lila's hand. "Look!" she cried. "Look at the banner over the door!"

CONGRATULATIONS, JOHANNA AND LILA the banner read. YOU MAKE A GREAT TEAM!

"This story is incredible," Elizabeth said with a sigh, putting down her copy of the *Sixers*. "You did a really great job of researching and reporting. You did a great job of storytelling, too. It's like a novel."

Amy sat on the edge of Elizabeth's bed, smiling. "I'm glad you like it."

"Like it!" Elizabeth exclaimed. "I *love* it. It's got everything: mystery, comedy, music, betrayal, heroism, friendship. It's great. You've interviewed every single person involved, and you haven't made anybody into a villain. In their own way, everybody involved acted like a hero. And I think that's nice. I also think it's nice that you didn't write anything about Janet's night gear."

A snort of laughter escaped Amy. "I didn't really think it was in the public's best interest to print that. I didn't think it was in *my* best interests either. Janet would have killed me."

"I still can't believe I missed so much excitement," Elizabeth said. "I've been out sick for a week and a half, but I feel like I've been gone for a month. I'll be glad to get back tomorrow."

"And I'll be glad to hand the paper back over to

you," Amy said. "I don't think I'm ready to step into your shoes yet—or Carl Birnbaum's."

"Come on, Amy! What are you talking about? You did an incredible job," Elizabeth protested.

Amy shook her head and laughed.

Elizabeth snapped her fingers. "Hey, before I forget. I promised a while ago that one of us would cover the life-saving course they're giving at the Sweet Valley community pool next week."

"Why don't you sign up to take the course?" Amy suggested. "Then you could write about it from an insider's perspective."

"That's a great idea," Elizabeth agreed. "I'll sign up tomorrow, right after school." She shrugged. "After all, you never know when life-saving skills may come in handy."

How will Elizabeth use her life-saving skills? Find out in Sweet Valley Twins and Friends #74, **ELIZABETH THE HERO.**

☎

1 (800) I LUV BKS!

If you'd like to hear more about your
favorite young adult novels and writers . . .
OR
If you'd like to tell us what you thought
of this book or other books
you've recently read . . .

CALL US at 1(800) I LUV BKS
[1(800)458-8257]

You'll hear a new message about books and
other interesting subjects each month.

**The call is free to you, but please get
your parents' permission first.**